™

FiRE & iCE

Adapted by Michael Anthony Steele

SCHOLASTIC INC.

New York Toronto London Auckland Sydney
Mexico City New Delhi Hong Kong Buenos Aires

Published by Scholastic Inc. SCHOLASTIC and associated logos are trademarks and/or registered trademarks of Scholastic Inc.

ISBN 0-439-78781-5

12 11 10 9 8 7 6 5 4 3 2 1   6 7 8 9 10/0
Printed in the U.S.A.
First printing, April 2006

CHAPTER 1

The cold air blew through Icy's long, white hair as she soared toward Cloud Tower. Stormy flew on Icy's left, a dark cyclone trailing behind her. On Icy's right, soared Darcy. Sparks of electricity danced over her thin body.

This is going to be good, thought Icy. She couldn't wait to see the look on Professor Griffin's face. *Expel us, will she?* Icy poured on the speed. *We'll see who does the expelling this time!*

The three witches dove through menacing clouds. The dark spires of Cloud Tower School for Witches came into view. Winding stairs and twisting buttresses sprouted from the structure and converged on the thick central tower. The crimson glow from the tower's windows brightened as they approached.

"Should I rip off the roof?" asked Stormy, eyes gleaming.

"That would make quite an entrance," smirked Darcy.

"No," said Icy. "Let's walk through the front door like we own the place." A wicked grin stretched across her face. "After all, in about five minutes, we *will* own the place!"

The witches cackled as they lightly touched down in front of the giant wooden doors. Icy waved a hand and the heavy doors swung open. She led the way as they strolled down the short passageway toward the main chamber.

The echoing clicks of their boot heels were slowly overpowered by the growing murmur of voices. As they stepped into the main chamber, Icy realized that they had timed their arrival perfectly. The entire student body was assembled for dinner. Student witches sat at each of the tables. The tables sat on platforms that jutted out of the tower walls. A spiral staircase wound around and up the tower. It connected the platforms and led to the highest balconies — where the faculty sat.

A hush fell over the students as the three witches entered. Icy could hear whispers from the girls on the lower platforms.

"Oh my darkness!" one student witch said. "Look who just showed up!"

Another girl gasped. "They're the seniors who got expelled!"

"What's the meaning of this?" boomed a voice from the highest balcony. Professor Griffin leaned over the railing and scowled at the three witches. "I made it perfectly clear that you were not to set foot on this campus!" Her eyes blazed on each side of her pointed nose.

The older woman's robe fluttered as she seemed to gather energy. She jutted both palms toward the witches and launched a green bolt of energy. The beam widened as it approached the girls, but they did nothing. Finally, the beam expanded to create an imprisoning dome over the three witches.

Icy laughed. "Nice try, teach."

"But things are a little different now," added Darcy.

"Show her what's up, Icy!" said Stormy.

Icy stepped toward the swirling dome of energy. She gently touched the glowing barrier with her palm. Suddenly, the green dome crackled as it turned to ice. The dome burst and hundreds of shards of ice spun toward the top of the tower. They blasted Griffin backward and onto the ground.

"How dare you!" she yelled. Two of the other teachers ran to her aid.

"Professor Griffin!" shouted Miss Ediltrude.

"Are you alright?" asked Miss Zaratustra. She turned toward the girls. "This behavior is unacceptable!"

"What are you going to do?" asked Darcy with raised eyebrows. "Give us detention?" The three of them laughed as Professor Griffin slowly got to her feet.

"Teach the teachers a lesson, Stormy!" Icy ordered.

Stormy's eyes glowed amber and lightning danced off her frizzy hair. She gathered energy, and then spread her arms wide. A dark tornado appeared in the center of the tower. The mighty winds snatched the students out of their chairs and spun them about. The two teachers raised their hands preparing to cast a counterspell. But before they could say a word, the tip of the tornado swooped them up and flung them through two of the tower windows. Stormy laughed as she returned her hands to her side. The tornado disappeared and the students began to plummet.

"Help!" screamed one of the girls.

"I'm coming!" shouted Griffin. She leapt off the balcony and shot a beam of energy at the nearest group of students. "*Softurius Landus!*" The girls disappeared, and then safely reappeared on the floor below. "*Cushionus Fallus!*" Griffin shouted as she saved another group of students. Then, still falling, she spread her arms wide. "*All Encompassus!*" The rest of the students disappeared, and then rematerialized on the ground.

As she continued to fall, Professor Griffin turned her gaze to Icy, Darcy, and Stormy. "You girls are finished!" she yelled. Then Griffin disappeared in midair.

Icy heard the rustle of cloth over her shoulder. She knew the professor had materialized behind her. She casually turned her head and saw that the woman had created a giant banishing ball. The burning white sphere of light was one of the most powerful spells a witch could conjure.

Professor Griffin growled as she sailed the ball toward Icy. Before it could hit its target, Darcy stepped in its path and caught it with both hands. The professor stared in disbelief as Darcy forced the ball down to the size of a small marble. The young witch glared at Griffin through a few loose strands of her long, brown hair. Then, between two fingers, she popped the tiny ball as if it were a grape.

Griffin's eyes widened. "That's impossible!" she shouted. "No one can do that!"

"Oh, that's nothing," sneered Stormy.

The three witches took a step toward the professor. Together, they extended their arms and gathered energy.

"Wait until you feel the full force of the Dragon Fire," said Darcy.

The professor raised a defensive arm. "What?"

The three witches laughed as they shot a blast of energy at the professor. The woman flew across the chamber and slammed against the wall.

"It looks like you're taking an early retirement," Stormy yelled.

Icy felt exhilarated as she gathered energy for the final blow. She never felt so powerful.

CHAPTER 2

Bloom never felt so powerless. Her hands shook nervously, rattling the small teacup and saucer. It was as if she didn't even have the strength to hold something that small. With her head tilted down, her long, red hair formed a protective barrier between her and everything in the headmistress's office. She glanced up through some of her strands of hair. Headmistress Faragonda and Professor Griselda watched her patiently. They waited to hear her story.

How could she tell them? She had just found out that she possessed some of the strongest fairy magic in all the realms — the Dragon Fire. And just as she became aware of its potential, it was stolen.

"Drink it while it's hot, dear." Miss Griselda nodded toward the teacup in Bloom's hand. "It'll make you feel better." The head of discipline's usual scowl was replaced by a genuine look of concern.

"Now then," said Headmistress Faragonda. "Why don't

you tell me everything that happened." She wore her usual concerned expression. The older woman had always been very kind to Bloom.

Bloom took a sip of the warm tea. Surprisingly, it did have a slight calming effect. "I was thinking of quitting Alfea," she began.

"What do you mean?" asked the headmistress.

"I didn't feel like I belonged," replied Bloom. "I went back home, to Earth."

Up until a few months ago, Bloom had no idea that fairies, witches, or even magic existed at all. She was just a regular Earth girl. Then she met Stella, and all of that changed. Bloom discovered that she possessed magical powers. She discovered that she, herself, was a fairy. Back on Earth, however, she had learned that she was much more.

"I found out who I really am and where I came from." Bloom set the cup and saucer on Miss Faragonda's desk. "I'm a member of the Royal Family of Sparks." She sighed. "I guess that's cool and all, but I am the only one left!"

Miss Faragonda and Miss Griselda exchanged glances. Bloom wasn't sure if they believed her, but she continued anyway. "Apparently, I am the keeper of a power called the Dragon Fire!"

Faragonda leaned back in her chair and adjusted her glasses. "Yes, I suspected as much."

Bloom's eyes widened. "You knew something about this?" she asked. "Why didn't you say anything to me?"

"I wanted to, Bloom." The headmistress sighed. "But

I've always believed that the truth comes to us when we are ready to hear it."

Bloom's anger grew. "Maybe, but I *wasn't* ready to hear it!" She stood and paced behind her chair. "Especially not from those three witches!"

"What three witches?" asked Griselda. "What are you talking about?"

Bloom could feel her eyes welling with tears. "Icy, Darcy, and Stormy followed me to Gardenia," she replied. "They're the ones who told me everything! They attacked me, and . . ." Bloom stifled a sob. "And they took the Dragon Fire!" Bloom brushed a tear from her cheek as she tried not to relive the entire wretched event. "They said they were going to use it to summon some magical army or something."

Griselda gasped. "Not the Army of Decay!"

"That's it!" said Bloom. "What does that mean?"

Miss Faragonda leaned forward and put her face in her hands. "It means the entire realm is in grave danger."

CHAPTER 3

Later, back in the dorm, Stella gazed at a very sad sight indeed. With her head hung low, Bloom sat in the center of her bed. Her friends, Flora, Tecna, and Musa, sat silently around her. Stella stood beside the bed and surveyed the situation. Normally, Flora's plants and flowers made her and Bloom's room one of the most beautiful rooms in Alfea. Now, with five teenage girls moping about, it looked more like a funeral parlor.

Finally, Bloom broke the silence. "I hate this!" She punched her pillow. "I just . . . I wish I'd never discovered my Winx or come to Alfea!"

"You can't mean that," said Stella. Normally, the blonde princess of Solaria would add a bit of stinging satire or an egotistical idiom. Now, she just moped with the rest of them.

"I do," Bloom replied. "That way, the witches never would've found me and stolen the power." She wiped away another tear. "And no one would be in danger."

"It's hardly your fault," said Tecna. "It was three against one, after all." She always had a logical way of looking at things.

"That's right," said Flora in her melodious voice. She placed a comforting hand on Bloom's shoulder. "You can't blame yourself."

"Seriously," added Musa. Even her perky, dark pigtails seemed to droop a little.

Bloom got up and walked over to Kiko. The little, gray-and-white rabbit sat in his bed, nibbling a carrot. Bloom picked up Kiko and gave him a hug. "I just wish I knew what to do," she said. As if sensing her despair, the small bunny nuzzled his nose under her chin.

Just then, the phone chirped. Stella picked it up on the first ring. "Bloom and Flora's room," she said. "How may I help you?"

"Hi, Stella," said a familiar and somewhat nervous-sounding voice. "Is, uh, Bloom there?"

Stella tightened her lips into a scowl. It was Brandon. No, that wasn't right. His *real* name was Sky. It turned out that the boy Bloom was seeing had been lying to her the whole time. He had traded places with his squire named Brandon, but his real name was Prince Sky of Erakleon. And not only had he been lying, but it turned out that he was engaged to a snotty princess named Diaspro.

Stella turned away from the others and spoke quietly. "I'm sorry," she said in the coldest voice she could muster. "Bloom is unavailable right now."

"Would you give her a message for . . ."

"Gotta go now, Brandon," Stella interrupted. "Or Prince Sky or whoever you are!"

She grimaced as she turned off the phone. Stella had just started seeing the boy she *thought* was Prince Sky. Now, she knew that she was involved with a lowly squire named Brandon. She hoped no one in the royal circles found out.

Oh, well, she thought. *At least Sky won't be bothering Bloom today.* She was suffering enough as it was.

CHAPTER 4

As Riven tightened the last coil on his levabike, he peered over the seat at Prince Sky. He had watched as the blonde boy called and asked to speak to Bloom. Riven smiled as Sky had obviously been shot down. The prince hung his head as he placed his phone in his pocket and trudged toward the Red Fountain dorms.

"Trouble in loser paradise," Riven said to himself. He zipped up his tool pouch and placed it into the bike's storage compartment. "Darcy will love this!"

Riven placed his helmet over his spiked hair and hopped onto his bike. It started with a satisfying hum and rose a foot off of the ground. Riven turned the handlebars and drove it through the front gate. Within seconds, his levabike zoomed away from the Red Fountain School for Heroics and Bravery and toward Cloud Tower and his crush, Darcy.

Riven had first met Darcy at the Day of the Rose annual levabike race. Ever since then, he couldn't take his mind off her. All of his so-called friends tried to tell him that Darcy was an evil witch, but he didn't listen. In fact, he planned to get back at them for the nasty things they said. So when Darcy asked him to spy on Prince Sky and Bloom, he gladly accepted. He tackled his new assignment with great vigor. For whenever he had something to report, it was a chance to speak to Darcy. And whenever he could, he took the information directly to her. It was a chance to *see* Darcy. They made the perfect couple. They even came up with cute code names for each other.

As Cloud Tower came into view, Riven hit the transmit button on his helmet. "Puppy Dog to Stiletto," said Riven. "Requesting permission to enter Cloud Tower."

"Permission granted," said Darcy. "Come on in."

Riven flew up the ramp leading toward the main gate. The dark castle seemed gloomier than ever. There was no one on the balconies and all of the windows and doorways were dark — except one.

Darcy stepped out of the lit doorway and onto the large balcony. "Over here, Puppy Dog!" she said as she waved.

Riven pulled back on the handlebars and soared toward her. He circled around, and then brought the levabike to a gentle stop on the balcony. Throwing off his helmet, he marched into the large room.

"Why didn't you call me back last night?" asked Riven. He glanced around what appeared to be a large office. Icy sat behind a wooden desk while Stormy stood nearby.

"I've been busy," said Darcy as she strode to the back of the room.

"Too busy for me?" asked Riven.

Icy and Stormy cackled loudly. Darcy spun around and smirked. "I hope I didn't hurt your little feelings."

Suddenly, the balcony door slammed shut. "Hey, what's going on here?" asked Riven.

"I was going to ask you the same thing," said Darcy. "You here to take me on another date?"

Riven's cheeks warmed. He scratched the back of his head nervously. "Well, I was hoping to, yeah." Icy and Stormy laughed louder as they moved toward Riven. The three witches formed a triangle around him. "But, I'm not sure I like what's happening here."

Stormy stepped up to Riven and ran a cold finger down his cheek. "You lost little boy," she said with a wicked gleam in her eye. "Don't you realize that no one cares what *you* like?" She jerked her hand from his face, scratching him with one of her long fingernails.

Riven winced. "Hey!"

Icy crossed her arms and glared at him. "You should've stuck with dating pixies."

"Haven't you heard, Riven?" asked Darcy. Her eyes flashed scarlet. "Witches make really bad girlfriends."

The three witches rose off of the ground and began to circle him. Their eyes glowed and they laughed louder than ever.

"Come on!" yelled Riven. "Stop messing around! This isn't funny!"

"You're wrong," said Icy. "It's absolutely hilarious!"

The witches spun faster and raised their hands above their heads. Sparks flew from their fingertips as books and sheets of paper whipped through the air. Riven stumbled as the floor shifted beneath his feet.

"In case you hadn't figured it out," said Darcy, "I'm breaking up with you!"

"So long, little boy!" yelled Icy.

Riven looked down to see the floorboards disappear into a black, swirling vortex. He remained suspended above it just long enough to look up at Darcy's face. The girl he had fallen for wore a twisted grin of delight. It was almost more than he could take.

"Darcy!" he yelled as he fell into darkness.

Hunger.

As Icy watched the vortex swirl into nothingness she felt ravenous. However, no food would satisfy this appetite. Icy was hungry for power. The defeat of Professor Griffin was a nice appetizer. The banishment of Riven cleared her palette. Now, she was ready for the main course.

"It's time to summon up the Army of Decay," she announced. With a wave of her hand, Professor Griffin's desk and bookshelves flew across the room as if they were nothing more than dollhouse furniture. Icy sat down on the restored wooden floor. "Complete the circle!" she ordered.

Darcy and Stormy sat across from her and across from each other. This time, they formed a much smaller triangle. They reached out and held each other's hands.

"Just feel that tremendous power flowing through you!" said Icy. The three witches began to glow. "This is the moment we've been waiting for. Are you ready?"

"You know it!" Darcy beamed.

"Bring it on!" Stormy agreed.

Icy smiled. "Begin the incantation."

The girls closed their eyes and began to chant in unison.

The young witches fell into a trance as they chanted the incantation over and over and over again.

Icy opened her mind's eye. As if floating above, she could see the three of them sitting on the floor. Tendrils of crimson light emerged from the witches' glow. They snaked away from them and disappeared through the office walls. As if in a dream, Icy willed herself to follow. She passed through the walls and saw the tendrils bend and twist into the moist soil. Once inside, lightning flashed and the mud began to bubble.

The ground around the castle churned faster. Then millions of tiny black insects burst from the soil. The decay bugs were like slimy worms with legs and claws. Their chatter was deafening.

*Tik-a-tik-a-tik-a-tik-a-tik-a-tik-a-tik-a-tik-a-tik-a-
tik-a . . .*

The bugs clambered over each other until they formed
a thick, squirming mass. Then each mass took shape to
form giant beasts. Icy recognized one of them immediately.
They were the mythological rot monsters. Hard shells ran
up their backs leading to their jagged heads. Their long
snouts ended with round mouths packed full of squirming tentacles. Each of their long arms ended with a
snapping claw.

The scrambling insects formed larger beasts as well.
Giant headless berserkers grew from the tallest mounds of
slime bugs. They pounded their gorilla-like fists into the
ground in defiance.

High above, other decay insects had joined to form flying beasts. They floated through the sky like stingrays
floating through the sea. Each of them screamed through
round, teeth-filled mouths.

Icy was pulled back from her vision by Stormy's voice.
"How big an army are we going to get, Icy?" Stormy
asked.

Icy opened her eyes. "Hard to say," she replied. "But
every molecule of decay from the last millennium will rise
up and become one of our soldiers!"

Their incantation complete, the three witches cackled
wildly as they stood and opened the office doors. They
stepped onto the balcony and gazed at the ground below.
Thousands of the disgusting creatures stood in formation

around the castle. They were awaiting orders. Hundreds of the stingrays circled overhead.

"We were popular before," said Darcy, "but we never had this many followers!"

"Yeah," Icy agreed. "This is going to be so awesome!"

CHAPTER 5

Bloom had begun to feel a little better. Talking things over with her friends always helped. She was about to ask their advice about Prince Sky when Flora stood and went to the window.

"What's going on out there?" asked Flora.

The other girls joined her. The sky darkened as black clouds enveloped the blue sky. After a flash of lightning, it began to rain.

Tecna leaned closer. "That's strange."

"What is?" asked Stella.

Tecna tapped the glass. "Those are Syridul Clouds."

"And that means?" asked Stella.

"I'm not sure," Tecna replied. "All I know is that the current air pressure wouldn't allow Syridul Clouds to form."

The fairies in the courtyard scattered as the rain became heavier. Then Bloom noticed that they were scattering for a different reason. "What is that down there?" she asked.

As if the rain were made of oil, a dark pool appeared in

the courtyard below. It churned and swirled as if it were alive. Bloom could also hear a faint rhythmic noise she'd never heard before.

Tik-a-tik-a-tik-a-tik-a-tik-a-tik-a-tik-a-tik-a-tik-a-tik-a . . .

"I don't know what that is," said Stella as she pointed toward the dark mass. "But I think we're about to find out!"

The girls watched as the darkness crept up the side of their dorm building. The ticking sound grew louder. When it reached their window, they saw exactly what it was — millions of black insects.

"They're, like, little bugs or something," said Musa.

They didn't look like any bugs Bloom had seen before. They looked more like slimy worms with spider legs. The disgusting creatures scraped at the glass with tiny claws.

"They're trying to break in!" screamed Tecna.

"Get back!" Bloom yelled.

As the girls stepped away from the window, the glass shattered inward. The insects poured through the opening. They began to cover the room from floor to ceiling. Their creepy sound was louder than ever.

TIK-A-TIK-A-TIK-A-TIK-A-TIK-A-TIK-A-TIK-A-TIK-A-TIK-A-TIK!

"Extermination spell, please!" Stella yelled as she backed away from the disgusting mass.

The bedroom door burst open behind them. It was Professor Palladium. "Quickly, girls, get out of there!" The

Elfin teacher motioned them to follow. "We're evacuating the East Wing!"

Bloom grabbed Kiko and followed her friends out of their dorm rooms. Once in the hallway, they joined a river of frightened students as they ran toward the main stairs. They ran down the wide stairway and out the main doors.

"They're all over the courtyard!" yelled one of the students.

Another girl ran by with a few insects caught in her hair. "Get off me!"

Bloom and her friends watched as the bugs covered the building behind them. Pools of the insects bubbled up from the ground around them. Before long, they would cover everything.

"We can't just let a bunch of bugs overrun our school!" said Tecna.

"Yeah," said Musa. She stomped one of them with her foot. "Let's show these creepy crawlers some Winx!"

Bloom squeezed Kiko tighter. "But I don't have my powers."

Stella placed a hand on Bloom's shoulder. "Don't worry, Bloom. We've got this one covered."

Bloom smiled. "You're the best, Stella."

Stella stepped back. "Let's go, girls!"

Bloom watched as her four best friends transformed into fairies. They extended the first two fingers on each hand and crossed their arms. Magical sparks washed over them, transforming their clothes into dazzling outfits. Suddenly, Musa wore crimson boots with a matching short skirt with a sheer midriff. Flora's clothes transformed into a flowing pink skirt. Tecna became magically dressed in a sparkling purple jumpsuit. Fairy wings sprouted from each of their backs.

Once Stella was dressed in her stunning yellow two-piece, she took off her ring and tossed it into the air. With a flash, it transformed into a long, golden scepter. A round sun symbol adorned the top.

Stella flew high into the air. "Okay, bugs, say hello to the power of Solaria!" She pulled back the staff as if it were a long club. "Sun Sweeper!" she shouted as she swung the staff. As it cut through the air, it created a blinding arc of light. The blast shot toward the ground and slammed into a large cluster of insects. It peeled them off of the ground, and destroyed them in a burst of sparkles.

Musa flew over another giant mass of bugs. "Boogie Blaster!" she yelled, throwing a glowing ball of light through the air. The ball turned into a giant disco ball and hovered over another mound of churning bugs. As it spun in mid-air, it shot pounding pulses of light toward the creatures.

Flora flew across the courtyard toward a towering mass of insects. "Venus Gobbler!" she yelled as she tossed her own ball of light. The orb struck the ground just behind the menacing mass. The ground rumbled and a giant Venus fly-trap burst from the soil. It swallowed the bugs in one bite.

Bloom noticed that the rest of the students had transformed into fairies as well. Together, all of Alfea was battling the invading insects. "Don't worry, Kiko," she said as she stroked her frightened rabbit. "A bunch of little bugs aren't going to do anything. . . ."

Before Bloom could finish, a mass of insects sprouted from the ground and loomed over her. She stepped back, expecting the scuttling insects to leap toward her. Instead, the pillar of squirming bugs did something worse. They quickly transformed into a giant beast. The creature was slimy, like the insects, and bigger than an ogre. Slurping tendrils flailed out of its long snout. It looked down at Bloom with deep red eyes.

The beast reached forward with one of its massive claws. Bloom didn't wait around to see if it wanted to dance. Holding Kiko tightly, she ran back into the main hall. Unfortunately, she found herself facing an even bigger creature — a giant Pharaoh Lizard. She had seen pictures of them in her Enchanted Creatures class.

"Step aside, Bloom!" ordered the lizard. "I'll protect you."

Bloom recognized that voice. As she dashed to the far wall, she realized that the lizard was actually Professor Wizgiz. The short gnome was a master shape-shifter.

The floor shook as the professor charged toward the slimy beast. The lizard rammed the creature and it exploded into a thousand writhing insects.

"Thanks, Professor!" shouted Bloom.

The giant lizard turned to Bloom and winked. "I wouldn't want to lose one of my favorite students!"

The professor galloped outside to join the battle in the courtyard. Bloom followed and saw fairies hovering everywhere. Beams of light crisscrossed as they battled the enemy below. Bloom wished she had her powers so she could help her friends and fellow students. Luckily, it appeared that the fairies of Alfea were doing just fine. Slowly, the insects and giant tongue beasts were being destroyed.

CHAPTER 6

Sky's mind wasn't on his drills. Due to his training, however, he kept perfect pace with his fellow students. Master Codatorta barked a cadence as they marched in formation. Their long capes fluttered over their pressed blue-and-white uniforms. Unfortunately, Sky's thoughts were on someone else — Bloom.

He should have told her the truth. He should have told her that he and Brandon had switched identities. But that was all part of it, wasn't it? Sky wanted to become someone else. He wanted to feel what it was like to be a regular person and not the prince of Erakleon. Therefore, he had agreed to pretend Brandon was the prince and *he* was a simple squire. For all he knew, Bloom may not have wanted to go out with him if she thought he was some stuck-up prince. Unfortunately, he didn't give her the chance to make that decision for herself.

Then there was Diaspro. Sky winced at the thought of

her. He was so caught up with Bloom, he had completely forgotten about his arranged marriage to Princess Diaspro. The marriage had been planned since his birth, so he never really thought of her romantically. One thing was for certain; he didn't plan to go through with it. He didn't know how he would tell his parents, but he was calling off the marriage.

Sky was ripped from his thoughts by the sound of the alarm. Master Codatorta held up a hand, instructing them to halt. The stout, bearded man looked up to the east wall as a sentry ran into view.

"Creatures approaching from sky and land!" the sentry announced. The young boy's face was ashen. "They're nearly at the east gate! Hundreds of them!"

"They're at the west gate too," yelled a voice behind them. Sky and the others turned to see another sentry standing on the west wall.

"And the South!" yelled another voice.

"Don't worry," said a boy next to him. "The barricades will keep them out."

Suddenly, hundreds of insects appeared at their feet. They poured out of the ground, from the cracks in the stone floor.

Tik-a-tik-a-tik-a-tik-a-tik-a-tik-a-tik-a-tik-a-tik-a-tik-a . . .

"To arms!" yelled Master Codatorta. He extended his energy bullwhip. "To arms!"

Immediately, every Red Fountain boy activated his energy

weapon. Some used blazing sharp spears, while a few fought with energy battle claws. Even though they were young, all of them were schooled in combat.

Sky activated his personal energy sword and shield. For a moment, he wondered how he would battle an army of insects with a sword. He might be better off squashing them with his shield. His question was quickly answered. A swarm of bugs in front of him transformed into a vicious monster. The creature had large shells on its back and two large claws.

Sky didn't wait for introductions. He reared back, then slashed his sword clean through the rot monster. Sliced in half, the ugly beast toppled over. It reverted to a mass of squirming bugs when it hit the ground. They writhed, then disappeared back into the ground.

"Good one, Prince Sky!" said a voice behind him.

Sky turned to see his squire and best friend, Brandon. The brown-haired boy chopped at a creature of his own.

"Thanks," said Sky.

Nearby, their friend Timmy had a monster charging right at him. "Come on, you slime!" he yelled defiantly. "Charge at this!" Timmy blasted the beast with his energy pistol. The monster howled as it disintegrated into writhing insects.

As he fought, Sky was amazed how easily these creatures were defeated. However, their strength was in their numbers. It seemed as if every time one was struck down, two would take its place.

"Take that!" yelled Master Codatorta as he wrapped the end of his whip around a creature's neck. He gripped the whip with both hands and jerked the monster off its feet. It flew over their heads and slammed into two more rot monsters.

"There are too many of them!" yelled one of the boys. "We can't keep this up!"

"Look!" yelled Brandon. "Up there!"

Sky looked up to see a small rectangular ship hovering above the courtyard.

"What is it?" asked Timmy. "Reinforcements?"

The side hatch slid open and three armored guards stepped to the edge. Armed with pulse rifles, they aimed at the creatures below. Just then, a familiar face leaned into view. A young girl with long, blonde hair glanced at the battle below. Then she turned to the guards.

"Fire!" Diaspro ordered.

Golden bursts of energy blasted from the rifles and streamed into the battle below. They ripped through every monster in the immediate area. Sky's own foe exploded as the shots riddled through it.

Diaspro pointed to Sky. "There he is!"

One of her guards threw down a rope. The knotted line dangled a few feet in front of Sky.

"Grab the rope, my prince!" Diaspro shouted. "We're getting you out of here!"

"What?" asked Sky. He couldn't believe his ears.

"We're here to rescue you!" she shouted. "This army is endless. Red Fountain will fall!"

Sky glanced around at his fellow students. They bravely battled the invading creatures. He turned back to Diaspro. "Then I will fall with it!" he shouted. "My place is here!"

Diaspro's eyes widened. "Don't be absurd," she said. "You're a prince! You have a higher calling!" She stared at him for a moment while the guards continued to blast the monsters around him. "Now, grab the rope!" she ordered.

Sky had to make a choice. He looked into her eyes and decided the choice was quite simple. He stepped toward the rope and slashed off the end with his sword. "My friends need me more!" he yelled up to her.

Princess Diaspro scowled at Sky, and then turned to the guards. "Leave him!"

The soldiers ceased firing and stepped back. The door slid shut and the ship rose into the clouds.

"Help!" shouted one of the freshmen students. A rot monster had him pinned. As Sky slashed the monster in two, he knew he had made the right decision.

CHAPTER 7

After the attack, the girls of Alfea didn't quite know what to do. They had fended off a particularly disgusting foe, but now what? Should they go back to class? Chances were that most of the classrooms were in disarray. Many of the girls began to clean up their school. Others gathered and talked about what they'd do if there was another attack. Bloom decided that their enemy had to be stopped from the source.

She ran up the stairs and down the hall to Miss Faragonda's office. Bloom had to convince the headmistress to let her do something to get her power back. After all, if Icy, Darcy, and Stormy didn't have Bloom's Dragon Fire, then they wouldn't be able to summon the Army of Decay.

As Bloom approached the headmistress's office, she heard voices on the other side of the open door. Bloom peeked in to see Miss Faragonda and Professor Saladin, the headmaster of Red Fountain. The two school leaders scowled as they watched a projection of Icy, Darcy, and Stormy.

"Time to face the facts, professors," Icy sneered. "You don't have a chance against us. If you want your precious little school spared from total destruction, you must follow these conditions."

Stormy leaned forward. "First, lay down your arms and surrender . . . *unconditionally*."

"Second," Icy added, "I want all of you to stand in front of your students and say, *Icy rules! Icy's the greatest!* Then you have to swear allegiance to us."

Darcy grinned. "If you don't do that, then we're going to wipe your schools right off the face of the realm!"

"You have five hours to decide," Icy said. She waved her hand and the projection disappeared.

Faragonda sighed. "If those witches think we're just going to hand over our schools to them, they're crazier than I thought."

"Perhaps," said Saladin. "But they have the power of the Dragon Fire."

The headmistress sat in her chair. "There may still be a way to defeat them if Bloom is brave enough to undertake that special mission."

"Let's hope she is," Saladin grumbled. He moved to the center of the room. "I'll see to it that the witches attack Red Fountain first. That should buy you and your girls some time." He tapped his dragonhead staff on the floor. "But Bloom must be swift. I don't know how much more my students can take."

"Good luck, Professor Saladin," said Miss Faragonda.

The short, gray-haired man raised his staff above his head. He vanished in a puff of orange smoke.

Miss Faragonda smiled. "Did you get all of that, Bloom?"

Startled, Bloom swallowed hard. She gently pushed open the door and stepped into the office. "I'm sorry, Miss Faragonda. I was just coming to see you and . . ."

"That's quite all right," Faragonda interrupted. "As you heard, I'm going to send you on a special mission."

Bloom heard footsteps running down the hall.

"I'll tell you all about it as soon as your friends arrive," the headmistress continued. "This concerns them, too."

Just then, Stella, Musa, Flora, and Tecna burst into the room.

"Miss Faragonda, have you seen Bloo . . ." Musa began to ask. "Oh."

"Gather 'round, girls," Faragonda instructed. With puzzled expressions, the girls did as they were told. Miss Faragonda moved around to sit on the edge of her desk.

The headmistress told them about their conversation with the witches and the ultimatum. "Now, Red Fountain is going to try to draw the next wave of attacks."

"They are?" asked Stella.

"But it's only a diversion," Faragonda explained. "Once Red Fountain falls, the witches will turn their eyes back on us." She sighed. "Their forces will crash hard upon our walls, but an Alfea girl never gives up, no matter how slim the hope." She reached out and held Bloom's hands. "And you, Bloom, still hold the key to what little hope we have."

"I do?" asked Bloom.

"Yes," the headmistress replied. "If one candle is used to light another, the fire passes on, but the original flame still glows. Do you see?"

Bloom shook her head. She didn't have anything burning inside her. As far as her powers went, Bloom felt cold inside.

Miss Faragonda smiled. "They can take the fire from you, but they can't take your ability to burn. Since you are the last heir of the Royal Family of Sparks, you are the only one who can use the Dragon Fire to its full potential."

"But the witches have it now," Flora pointed out.

Faragonda turned to Flora. "Not all of it."

The headmistress stood and moved toward the girls. They stepped back as Faragonda extended her hands and a glowing orb rose from the floor. Inside was a projection of a beautiful green-and-blue planet.

"In its day, Sparks was the greatest of all worlds," Faragonda explained. "And the Dragon Fire was the source of its life."

Miss Faragonda flicked her wrist and the planet disappeared. An image of a beautiful castle appeared in its place. The castle was made of several slim towers, each ringed with golden trim and beautiful adornments.

The headmistress passed a hand over the globe and

the castle was soon covered with snow and ice. "But then that flame was extinguished, and the planet was cast into an eternal winter." She snapped her fingers and the globe blinked out of sight.

Bloom thought she understood. "So, since I'm the heir, I could go there, relight the flame, and reabsorb its power. Is that what you're saying?"

The headmistress turned to Bloom and looked her in the eyes. "It could be a very dangerous mission."

"Yeah, but we'll be with you, Bloom," said Musa.

"That's right!" Tecna agreed. "You can always count on us."

"No matter what, we've got your back!" added Stella.

Bloom smiled. "Thanks, guys."

CHAPTER 8

Bloom and her friends stood on the long catwalk stretching across the Magical Reality Chamber. This wasn't the first time Bloom had been in this particular part of the school. Occasionally, Professor Palladium used the chamber to simulate different planets and realms. The first time Bloom took a test in the chamber, the three witches sabotaged the controls. They made it to where they could project holographic versions of themselves into Bloom's simulation. Luckily, Bloom had been able to defeat them. She just hoped they didn't tamper with the controls this time.

"Can you hear me, girls?" asked Professor Palladium. His voiced sounded tinny coming from the chamber speakers. He waved from the control room. Through the glass, Bloom could see him along with Miss Faragonda and Miss Griselda.

"We hear you, prof!" Stella replied.

"Good," said the professor. "I've reprogrammed the

chamber to create a transdimensional corridor. It will transport you to Sparks."

"Ingenious," muttered Tecna.

"This is *not* virtual reality," Palladium continued. "The dangers you'll face will be quite real and most formidable. All sorts of nasty creatures inhabit dead planets. Unfortunately, we know nothing about most of them."

"That's comforting," whispered Musa.

"Now, stand still for me," instructed the professor. "Before we can send you, we have to suit you up in the appropriate attire."

Bloom watched as the professor pushed several buttons on the control panel.

"You see, the weather on Sparks is quite brutal," he continued. "So I'm afraid open-toe shoes and exposed midriffs simply won't do."

Suddenly, five tiny balls of light floated down from the ceiling. They circled the girls, and then hovered above each of them. Like five tiny eggs, the balls hatched open and projected a field of light over each girl. As the field traveled down their bodies, their clothes transformed into winter wear. When the transformation was complete, they each wore matching black coats, pants, and gloves. Amber goggles covered their eyes and fleece-lined hoods covered their heads.

"If I had my way, this would be the year-round dress code," Griselda's voice sounded over the speakers.

"Oh, Griselda," replied Miss Faragonda.

Stella turned to admire her new attire. "These outfits rock!"

"Here we go, girls," said Palladium. He pressed a few more buttons and the entire chamber began to hum. "Remember, the fate of the universe hangs on your success. Good luck!"

"Gee, no pressure," muttered Musa.

Bloom squinted her eyes as the chamber began to glow. The hum grew louder and the light grew brighter. Soon, Bloom felt as if she were floating in a white void. She clenched her eyes tightly.

When the humming faded, Bloom opened her eyes. They stood on the surface of a snow-covered planet. Bits of ice stung her cheeks as a frigid wind blew across the landscape.

"Wow," said Flora, "what a desolate place."

"Eternal winters will do that to a planet," Stella remarked.

Bloom glanced around. Unfortunately, everything looked the same. "We need to figure out where the palace used to be."

"Leave that to me," Tecna announced. She extended an open palm. "I'll use my nav system." A projection of the surrounding landscape appeared over Tecna's hand. Wireframe mountains circled five little yellow dots. A larger blue dot blinked on the other side of a small mountain range. "There it is," Tecna announced. "We go north."

CHAPTER 9

Sky stood at attention along with his fellow heroes of Red Fountain. The entire student body stood in the open quad. They were separated into their individual classes and all eyes were on their headmaster, Professor Saladin. Master Codatorta stood beside him.

"Gentlemen!" the short man began. "Our scouts report that the second invasion is on its way! You fought well the first time, but today it's time to put everything you've learned to the test." He raised his staff. "We may be out-numbered, but that does not mean we are outmanned!"

Codatorta raised a defiant fist. "For honor!"

The assembly of boys did the same. "And the glory of Red Fountain!" they shouted in unison.

Suddenly, the sky darkened as black clouds converged to a point above the school. Lightning flashed, thunder roared, and something much more frightening appeared — a giant projection of Stormy's head.

"Look at all the little boys in uniform!" she said with a sneer. "How pathetic!"

Stormy's image roared with laughter, and then disappeared. As she vanished, it began to rain the same oily raindrops as before. Soon, the ground rumbled and the familiar insect noise filled the air. The slimy worm-bugs erupted from the ground around them.

Tik-a-tik-a-tik-a-tik-a-tik-a-tik-a-tik-a-tik-a-tik-a-tik-a . . .

Master Codatorta activated an energy sword. "Hold steady!" he ordered. "Wait for my command!"

Sky pressed the button on his own energy sword. He heard a satisfying hiss as the dazzling blue blade erupted from the hilt. Soon everyone around him had their energy weapons ready.

"Remember the formations we learned in Advanced Tactics!" Codatorta reminded.

Black insects were everywhere. They gravitated toward each other, and then squirmed as several dark masses. The writhing forms rose and towered over the boys. Slowly, they transformed into the wicked rot monsters.

"Steady!" said Codatorta. "Homeroom A, circle around!" He took a step forward. "Homerooms B and C, push them back to the gates!"

Sky and the others charged the ugly beasts. Blazing swords, spears, whips, and hooks slashed through the creatures. Each one crumbled into a heap of disintegrating bugs.

Sky found himself surrounded by three of the monsters. He slashed one beast in two, and then flipped backwards as the other two jabbed at him with their enormous claws. Once back on his feet, he kicked a creature away from him while simultaneously slicing the other with a backhanded blow. The creature he kicked stumbled backwards. A crimson blade struck it from behind and it crumbled away. Brandon held the blade.

"Thanks!" said Sky.

Brandon squared off to another attacker. "Now, watch this move! It's my patented Overhead Slam Bash!" Brandon leapt into the air and brought his sword down on the monster's head like a hammer onto a nail. The beast split in two and disintegrated.

Brandon smiled proudly. His smile disappeared and his eyes widened. "Sky! To your right!"

Sky turned and raised his sword just in time. His blade blocked two nasty claws flying toward his head. He strained against his sword as he kept the beast from pushing him down. Its slimy tentacles squirmed inches from his face.

A yellow fist flew past his head and slammed into the face of the beast. The creature flew back into a wall. It exploded into wiggling insects.

Sky turned to see Knut standing behind him. Sky had first battled the yellow ogre in Bloom's backyard, on Earth. *What was he doing here?* Sky thought. *He worked for Icy, Darcy, and Stormy!*

Sky raised his sword, but Knut raised his hands in

defense. "Wait," yelled the ogre. "I'm on your side now! Icy wants to take over all the realms." He casually punched an approaching monster, and then continued speaking. "That includes the ogre realm and I have family back there!"

Timmy jumped between them. "Knut's cool," he said. "He's kicking some major monster butt!"

Sky was a bit hesitant in trusting Knut. Then again, the ogre was almost as big as the attacking monsters. And Knut *did* just save his neck.

"All right, then," said Sky. "Let's get these things!"

The three stood with their backs to each other and battled the surrounding beasts. Timmy fired his energy pistol at three of the slimy fiends. "Eat this, slimeball!" he shouted. "And this! And this!"

The three beasts crumbled into thousands of insects. However, this time, the bugs didn't disappear. Instead, they scrambled over each other to form a larger monster. It was the biggest beast any of them had faced so far.

The new berserker had broad shoulders and fists as big as boulders. It looked more like a two-story-tall, headless gorilla. Sky, Knut, and Timmy dove out of the way as the brute slammed its fists onto the ground.

"How do you stop these things?" asked Timmy.

CHAPTER 10

"**It is freezing!**" Bloom shouted over the howling wind. She wiped frost off of her goggles for the thousandth time. They all trudged through the knee-deep snow in a line behind Tecna. They were almost to the top of yet another hill.

Flora patted Bloom on the back. "Just find your inner warm place and keep walking."

"You find *your* inner warm place!" Stella barked. "Me, I'll take an extra blanket!"

"I think my inner warm place just fr-fr-froze," Musa said through chattering teeth.

"Come on, girls!" said Tecna. "Forward march! Or something."

When they reached the top of the hill, they paused to catch their breath. Unfortunately, the view from this hill looked the same as the view from the last five hills — a snow-covered wasteland with . . . more hills.

Stella pushed in between Bloom and Tecna. "We

should be close, shouldn't we?" She pointed to the horizon. "Maybe it's just beyond *that* hill?"

Just then, the ground shook beneath their feet. The distant hill shifted to one side, and then began to rise.

"Uh, I don't think that's a hill!" yelled Flora.

The ground rose higher and a gruesome face emerged. The hill wasn't a hill at all. It was the back of a giant snow monster. The towering giant stood to its full height, casting a long shadow over the girls. Bits of ice pelted them as it shook the snow off its back. It lifted its head toward the sky and let out a deafening roar. Two long tusks protruded from its tooth-filled mouth.

The girls screamed as the giant slammed its enormous fists against the ground. A tidal wave of snow washed over Bloom and her friends.

Buried in snow, Bloom couldn't use her powers to free herself. Feeling the ground shake, she quickly clawed her way to the top. It was clear that the giant snow beast was coming their way.

When she reached the surface, she saw that the others had climbed out as well. "Is everyone okay?"

"Yes," Tecna replied. "Let's get out of here!"

The girls ran back down the hill as the giant stomped after them. When they reached the bottom, they dashed into a small ravine. When the ravine forked, Tecna, Musa, and Flora took the left side while Stella turned right. She began to weave through a maze of jagged ice formations.

"Stay close to me, Bloom," Stella instructed.

Bloom followed Stella and the monster followed the others. Bloom and Stella ran until they reached a dead end.

"We're trapped!" yelled Stella.

The giant's footsteps grew louder as it doubled back. Soon its head came into view as it lumbered straight toward the two girls.

"I'm going to try and take this guy out!" Stella yelled. She leapt into the air and crossed her arms. "Sun Power!"

Golden light poured over her body as her snowsuit transformed into her yellow fairy outfit. Her delicate wings sprouted from her back.

Stella's hands glowed as she turned to the snarling beast. "Take this, you abominable abomination!" She blasted him with two shots of golden light. Yet, somehow, her magic seemed to just bounce off his furry pelt.

"I don't think he liked that," said Bloom.

Stella turned to Bloom. "Run! Get out of here!"

"No way!" Bloom yelled back. "I'm not ditching you!"

The giant roared as he grabbed one of the jagged ice formations. It broke from the ground leaving a sharp end. The beast reared back to throw it. The beast roared and flung the ice shard like a spear. Bloom and Stella dove away from each other as the chunk slammed into the frozen ground between them. Snow and ice flew everywhere and the ground trembled. Bloom stumbled to her feet as a giant crack appeared in the icy floor. The crack widened until a giant chasm formed at Bloom's feet.

"Bloom!" yelled Stella.

Bloom teetered on the edge of the chasm. She tried to keep her balance but it was no use. The ground shook harder, the chasm opened wider, and Bloom lost her footing. She fell into the darkness below.

CHAPTER 11

Icy cackled as she watched the mayhem. In Cloud Tower, the three witches gathered around a projection of Red Fountain. They gazed down in delight as their army of decay slowly overran the school.

"Beautiful," Icy purred. "No matter how much those fools fight, our army will continue to rise."

They watched as the boys struck down many of their multitongued rot monsters. As each beast fell, two more rose from the insects and took its place. If three or more were destroyed at once, a giant, headless berserker would form. The evil goliaths would smash everything in their path with their giant fists.

"Let's show these boys who rules," said Darcy.

"Yeah!" agreed Stormy.

Icy laughed louder. "It's time for Red Fountain to fall!" She turned her attention to the stables. Icy closed her eyes and concentrated on the stable's inhabitants. "Dragons of ice and fire, I am your master now! Break your shackles and descend upon my enemies!"

The three witches watched as the Red Fountain dragons strained against the chains. The tiny links snapped and a dozen of the winged beasts slammed through the stable doors.

One of the boys pointed to the creatures as they flew into the sky. "Up there! The dragons are loose!"

The dragons circled over the battlefields, then swooped toward the combatants.

Codatorta ducked as a red dragon snapped at his head. "They've been spelled!" he yelled. "Be careful!"

The witches laughed harder.

Prince Sky concentrated on the dragons above. He was at the top of his Dragon Wrangling class, but his skills weren't working now. The beast continued to swoop in and claw at his fellow students. Master Codatorta was right, the winged creatures were under a powerful spell. Plus, it wasn't easy to concentrate since he had to fight off monsters at the same time. He sliced off the arm of an attacking rot monster.

Sky turned his attention back to the dragon. Then he saw all the dragons scatter as the faces of the three witches appeared in the clouds. Stormy came back to gloat and she brought her witchy friends.

"What's the matter, boys?" asked Darcy. "Couple of girls too much for you?"

"Don't forget your dragons," Stormy added. "I guess they weren't so tame after all."

"And now, check out this dragon," said Icy. She closed her eyes and chanted, *"Dragon of Frost, spread your wings and fly!"* Her giant head blew an icy wind toward the battlefield. The wind took the form of an enormous ice dragon. Ten times the size of the other dragons, the new creature swooped in and coiled around all of Red Fountain. The temperature dropped twenty degrees as the dragon morphed into a dome of ice.

Sky heard a deafening crack. He looked up to see a fissure form in the middle of the tallest tower. The frozen structure broke free and slid away. It was sheared off completely.

Professor Saladin blasted a giant berserker with his staff. "We have no choice!" he yelled. "We must retreat!"

"Everyone, to the evacuation ships, now!" ordered Codatorta.

"Brandon, Timmy!" yelled Sky. "Help me cover their escape!"

The three fought off the few remaining monsters while the others ran to the hangar bay. They watched as red, wedge-shaped ships flew out the hangar doors and up through the opening in the ice.

Once the others had escaped, the three heroes made their way to the last ship. Timmy blasted giant berserkers as the others ran up the gangplank. Sky leapt into the control seat. He closed the hatch once Timmy was safely inside.

"Let's go!" Timmy yelled.

Sky powered up the ship and piloted it out of the hanger. He banked hard, just slipping through one of the berserker's grabbing hands. He pulled back on the stick and the ship shot straight up. Once they were clear of the ice, the ship continued to climb.

"Aren't we going to Alfea with the others?" Brandon asked.

"Not just yet," Sky replied. The clouds ahead gave way to the darkness of space.

CHAPTER 12

Bloom pulled herself off the ground. She was a little dizzy, but she wasn't hurt. Luckily, she had slid down several inclines on her way to the bottom of the chasm. She looked up to see only ice and a tiny crack of light, hundreds of yards away.

The light filtered down through the ice, so Bloom had a dim view of the cavern. Jagged icicles hung all around her, but there seemed to be a crude path winding between them. Bloom cautiously made her way through the ice.

"I have to find a way out of here," she said to herself.

As Bloom traveled, the tunnel widened. There was a bit more light and she could swear it was getting warmer.

Oh, what a cute baby, said a distant ghostly voice.

Bloom stopped in her tracks. "Who's there?" she asked.

It's time for your bottle, the voice replied. It was a woman's voice.

"Hello?" Bloom asked as she picked up her pace.

The cavern opened into the end of a long hallway. The

corridor was adorned with crumbling trim and rotting sconces. Faded tapestries hung on the walls.

The mysterious voice grew louder. *Rock-a-bye Princess, on your sweet throne, when you grow up, you'll rule on your own . . .*

"That voice sounds familiar," Bloom said.

Suddenly, Bloom's mind was filled with the vision of the hallway as it used to be. Extravagant fabrics decorated the shimmering chandeliers. The grand tapestries displayed images of a royal family. A kind-faced king smiled down at a red-haired baby in the queen's arms.

Excited, Bloom ran down the hallway and dashed up a set of stairs. She entered a long dining room. Ancient place settings still lined the long table. If not for the dust and cobwebs, the elegant dishes could have been placed there yesterday. "I think I've been here before."

Dinner is served, echoed a man's voice. *Everyone please be seated.*

Another vision flashed in Bloom's mind. She saw the dining room in its former glory. Golden utensils glistened, ornamental crystal sparkled, and fine foods covered the shiny white tablecloth.

"This is so weird," Bloom said as she crossed the room. "I remember this place." She pushed open two large doors and stepped into a grand reception hall. A domed ceiling stretched high over her head. "This was my home." Her eyes filled with tears. "This is the Sparks royal palace."

Suddenly, the ground shook and a crack appeared in

the ceiling. Bloom ducked under a large table as chunks of ice fell from above. She hoped the giant snow beast hadn't found her. A few more blocks smashed against the floor. Then, all was quiet.

"Oops," said Stella's voice from above. "I might have overdone it a bit."

"Oh, do you think so?" asked Tecna.

Bloom climbed out from under the table and saw her friends looking down through the large crack in the ceiling.

Flora pointed. "Look! It's her!" she yelled. "Hey, Bloom!"

"I am *so* glad to see you!" Bloom yelled back. "Come down and check out my palace!"

As the girls climbed down, they told Bloom how they had ditched the snow monster. Tecna had led them to the palace and Stella used the power of Solaria to defrost it. Once on the ground, everyone gazed around at the ancient castle. Unfortunately, Bloom's family palace didn't look so good.

"They really destroyed everything, didn't they?" asked Bloom.

Musa put a hand on Bloom's shoulder. "Yeah, but maybe not the Dragon Fire. I have this feeling that it's still here."

"You really think?" asked Bloom.

"Yeah, I do," Musa replied.

"Let's hope nothing is lurking down here," said Flora.

Tecna extended an open palm and a small wire-framed version of the castle appeared. "I don't detect any other life-forms." Part of the tiny castle glowed red. "Look at this." She pointed to the glow. "It's an undamaged area."

"It must have been protected by some really powerful magic," said Stella. "Like the Dragon Fire!"

"Maybe you're right and it's still here," said Bloom.

The girls followed Tecna's directions and made their way downstairs to another corridor. Although it was covered in dust, it was in much better shape than the rest of the castle.

Bloom, said a familiar voice.

"What was that?" asked Stella.

"I know that voice," said Bloom. "I think."

Tecna examined the readings on her projection of the castle. "We have a visitor, but it's not someone like us."

Just then, a bright glow filled the hallway. It slowly faded into a beautiful apparition before them. *Welcome, Bloom,* said a melodious voice. *I've been waiting for you.* The light took the shape of a beautiful woman. She wore a flowing, golden gown draped with beautiful shiny ribbons.

"Daphne!" said Bloom.

"You know her?" asked Musa.

"That's a great outfit," said Stella.

"She's the woman from my dream," Bloom explained.

"Maybe she's your fairy godmother or something," Stella suggested.

"Bloom," said Daphne. "Please, we must hurry." She turned and floated away from them. "Follow me!"

Bloom was excited. She had been dreaming about

Daphne ever since she got to Alfea. Unfortunately, every time Bloom wanted to ask her a question, the dream faded. Now, as they followed her down the long corridor, Bloom could ask whatever she wanted.

Daphne seemed to have sensed Bloom's first question. "I know the Dragon Fire was stolen," she said. "And you were right to come here to look for it."

"Will you show me where it is?" asked Bloom.

"Yes, but understand the flame is not hidden here on Sparks," said Daphne.

"It's not?" asked Bloom.

"No, but I have something else to show you." She stopped at the end of the hallway. A pair of ornate doors were guarded by two giant female statues on each side. Daphne waved a ghostly hand over the jewel-encrusted latches. The doors swung open. "This is the royal treasure room."

Mouths agape, the girls entered a room as big as their school's dining hall. It was filled with every type of treasure imaginable. There were piles of silver coins, heaps of diamonds and jewels, golden statues, and bolts of the finest silks and satins.

"Everything in this room is yours, Bloom," Daphne explained. "Take a look."

"Wow!" Bloom couldn't believe her eyes. "This is all mine?"

"It's yours," Daphne assured her.

The other girls were amazed as well. "Cool," said Flora.

"This is quite astonishing," said Tecna.

"Bloom can live large," Musa laughed. "This is what I call bling-bling!"

Stella placed her hands on her hips. "This is my kind of room!"

Daphne floated to a large pedestal in the center of the chamber. "Come here, Bloom."

Bloom and the others followed. "What is it?" asked Bloom.

Daphne gestured to an ornate pillow on the pedestal. "This belongs to you as well."

As Bloom moved closer, she saw a thin crown nestled in the center of the cushion. It was delicate like a tiara, and was elegantly encrusted with sparkling jewels.

"Whoa! I get a real crown?" asked Bloom.

"Yes," Daphne replied. "Pick it up. It will show you your story."

Bloom tentatively reached toward the thin crown. It seemed so fragile that she was almost afraid to touch it. She gently lifted it from the cushion and was surprised by its weight. There was something else as well — power. From the moment Bloom touched it, she felt an unseen force rush through her fingertips.

Suddenly, images poured into her mind. She saw a beautiful countryside. Rolling hills and stunning forests surrounded a grand castle. Bloom knew she was seeing Sparks.

"When you were born, Sparks was still filled with pure

55

magic," said Daphne. Her voice seemed to be coming from inside of her head. "But then the coven launched a sneak attack." Bloom saw three old crones hovering over the castle. They shot lightning, fire, and energy beams down at the people below. Bloom saw them run for their lives as the castle crumbled around them.

"They took over the entire planet and destroyed everything," Daphne continued. "What was once the most magical place in the universe became lifeless."

Bloom then saw Daphne. She wasn't ghostlike, but she was just as beautiful. She dodged falling debris as she carried something very small down a long corridor.

"The King called on me to save you and to guard the Dragon Fire," Daphne explained. "I sent you and the fire to the last place anyone would look for a magical creature."

Bloom saw that Daphne was holding a tiny baby — a baby with red hair. In the vision, Daphne waved a hand and a swirling portal appeared. She kissed the baby on the forehead, and then gently placed her into the vortex.

"I delivered you to Earth," Daphne continued. "It was the place where your destiny was waiting. A destiny that would nurture and care for you. It would prepare you to one day return to Sparks and reclaim your throne."

The images vanished. Bloom found herself looking at the crown through tear-soaked eyes. "I just can't believe this." She clutched it to her chest and fell to her knees. "I messed everything up."

Daphne knelt beside her. She placed a comforting arm

around Bloom's shoulder. "Don't cry. It's not your fault. You did what you could."

"But all of this happened so I could protect the Dragon Fire." Bloom wiped her eyes. "It was my responsibility and I let the witches take it. I didn't protect it at all."

Daphne gently stroked Bloom's head. "You will get the Dragon Fire back," she said. "It belongs to you. It is your destiny."

Bloom looked into the woman's glowing eyes. "Tell me what to do, Daphne." She stood and wiped away the remaining tears. "I'll do anything. I'll do whatever it takes to get the Dragon Fire back from those witches."

Daphne smiled and began to fade away. "Look for it, Bloom," she said. *Look for the Dragon Fire and you will find it.*

CHAPTER 13

"**So, *where* are** you supposed to look for it?" asked Flora.

"I don't know, but I'll find it," Bloom replied.

The girls walked out of the crumbling castle and into the cold landscape. The wind wasn't blowing as hard and one of the suns had come out. Bloom thought the barren setting was quite stunning in its own way. Although, when she got back the Dragon Fire, she would return to Sparks and try to restore its real beauty.

"Off topic," Stella chirped. "But what about all of the fabulous jewelry?"

Musa laughed. "I think Stella has her eye on a necklace or two."

Bloom smiled. "Okay, after I reclaim the throne, you can take your pick. But for now, let's pay a visit to those witches."

"Agreed!" said Stella.

"Absolutely!" said Tecna.

Bloom felt a rhythmic pounding under her feet. She looked up to see something moving on the horizon. She was about to ask what it was when it became obvious. The snow giant slowly lumbered into view.

"Uh-oh. Looks as if Mr. Abomination is back," said Stella.

As the beast topped the rise, Bloom saw hundreds of sparkling creatures skittering around his enormous feet.

"And he brought his posse!" Musa added.

The glistening animals had long, pointed heads and sharp tips on the ends of each of their four legs.

"Those are ice crabs," said Flora. "They can freeze fairies!"

Stella flew into the air. "Then let's make crab cakes. I know a great recipe!" She twirled her golden scepter. "Let's get cooking, girls!"

Bloom stepped back as Musa, Flora, and Tecna flew up to join Stella. They each crossed their arms and transformed into fairies. Once in their sparkling attire, they zoomed toward the approaching horde.

"So what's the recipe?" asked Flora.

"You can either deep-fry or broil them," Stella replied. "But first you have to crush them!"

"I can handle that with a sonic blast," said Musa. She closed her eyes and magical sound waves radiated from her body. The waves washed over the nearest group of crabs. The hissing animals vibrated off of the ground and floated in midair.

"I'll take care of the rest!" Flora blew on her open palm.

Magical clover leaves appeared and twirled beneath the crabs. When they hit the ground, large vines burst from the snow. "Pterodactyl vines, pulverize them!" Flora ordered. The vines coiled around most of the crabs and began to squeeze.

"They're ready, Stella," said Flora. "Turn on the heat!"

Stella twirled her scepter. "One order of melted ice crabs coming up!" Stella zipped down and slammed the end of her scepter onto the ground. A giant wave of heat blasted away from her and slammed into the ice crabs. They melted instantly.

"Nice!" said Flora. Just then, another wave of crabs skittered over the hill.

"No way!" said Stella. "There's more of them?"

Tecna's neon fairy wings morphed to a large glider wing. "I'll try Digital Deletion!" She zipped toward the attacking force with incredible speed. She zigzagged between them and emerged on the other side. Each crab she passed now wore a flashing microchip. "I just attach the chips, press delete . . ." She pushed a button on her glove and the crabs exploded. "And off they go to the great recycling bin in the sky!"

The giant snow beast bellowed in the distance. As if answering his call, another wave of ice crabs appeared on the ridge. They galloped down the hill toward the fairies.

"Look! There's more!" said Flora.

"There are far too many of them," said Tecna.

"Let's see if we can find cover in the castle!" said Bloom.

She ran through the castle doors as her friends flew in behind her.

"Those claws look nasty," said Stella. "They could really do some wardrobe damage!"

"I don't think you have to worry about that," said Flora. "One nip and you disappear!"

"Close the doors!" yelled Stella. She and Bloom slammed the huge doors. Just as they locked, several crabs bashed against the outside. The heavy doors cracked.

"We'd better move," suggested Tecna.

The girls ran toward the main hall. Unfortunately, several crabs were already there. They turned to go back only to see that they had been followed. The fairies were surrounded. Bloom grabbed an old torch from the wall and slammed it against two of the ice crabs. They shattered into ice cubes.

"Hey, your Earth power's pretty good," Stella joked.

"I don't think Earth power's going to get us out of this one," said Bloom.

"Here they come!" shouted Musa. Crabs poured through every opening in the main hall.

"I got it, girls!" exclaimed Flora. She spun around and dished out several sparkles of light. "These Extractor Seeds will take them out like a bad blackhead!" The seeds hit the ground in front of the approaching crabs. When the creatures moved closer, giant yellow flowers erupted from the ground and swallowed them whole. The flowers disappeared back into the floor.

"Very efficient!" said Tecna.

"Thanks, Tec!" said Flora.

A green ball of light appeared in Tecna's hands. "My turn!" She threw the ball at the nearest crab. The ball expanded into a round cage and sucked in the small monster. The ball spun around the floor, picking up four more ice crabs. When the cage was full, Musa blasted it apart with a crimson bolt of light.

"Good teamwork!" yelled Bloom.

"Bloom!" said Stella.

Bloom turned to see a crab heading straight for her. Its long, pointed head split open to reveal rows of jagged teeth. It hissed as it leapt into the air. Bloom froze. There was nothing she could do.

Suddenly, the crab split in two and disappeared. Standing where the crab had been was Prince Sky, his blue energy sword in his hand.

"Hi, Bloom," said Sky.

Brandon and Timmy dropped from the ceiling. With their weapons ready, they faced the approaching crabs.

"Don't worry girls, we're here!" said Brandon.

"We'll get you out of this!" Timmy added. Timmy blasted crabs with his pistol while Sky and Brandon ran straight into the approaching beasts. They sliced through the icy creatures with ease. From above, the rest of the fairies shot crabs with energy blasts. Soon, all the crabs were gone.

The castle shook.

"Did anyone feel that?" asked Tecna.

"Feel what?" asked Brandon.

The ceiling exploded above them. "That!" Tecna yelled. Everyone scattered as a giant fist slammed into the floor.

Sky and Brandon slashed at the monster's hand while Timmy shot it with his pistol. The giant roared and pulled his fist out of the castle. He didn't seem hurt. He seemed angrier.

"Uh-oh," said Sky.

"How are we going to beat this guy?" asked Timmy.

Stella smiled. "Don't worry, boys. We're here. We'll save you." She flew out through the hole in the ceiling. Flora and Musa followed.

"Hey, Tecna," yelled Bloom. "Why don't you use the World Wide Web to limit his movement?" asked Bloom.

"Great idea. I'll trap him." Tecna flew after the other girls.

Bloom and the boys ran out of the hall and through what was left of the front doors. She made it out just in time to see Tecna make the biggest energy web she'd ever created. It enveloped the beast in a giant ball.

"I'll plant some blast buds!" said Flora. She tossed a handful of buds toward the wire-frame sphere. They spread out and stuck all around it. "Can you give those buds a little sunshine, Stella?"

Stella's scepter glowed brightly. "Already on it!" She

waved it toward the ball and golden rays washed over the trapped beast. The tiny buds opened to reveal beautiful yellow flowers.

"Now to detonate!" said Musa. She spread her fingers wide and blasted the sphere with the deepest boom beat Bloom had ever heard.

As if sensing his demise, the giant gave a roar. Bloom squinted as the buds blew in a flash of blinding light. The giant flew backwards and landed in the deep snow. He was out cold.

"Monster booty has been kicked," Stella said proudly.

"Yeah!" Bloom yelled.

Sky was glad Timmy had agreed to pilot the ship on their journey home. He wanted to be alone with Bloom. He had a lot to talk about with her, but neither one of them had said a word so far. They just sat next to each other at the back of the ship. Sky was fearless in battle, but right then, he was terrified.

"Uh, Bloom?" he asked. "There's something I want to tell you."

"Yeah?"

He didn't know where to begin. "You see . . . this whole thing about really being Prince Sky and pretending to be Brandon . . ." He sighed. "I . . ."

Bloom crossed her arms. "Just tell me."

"Well . . . I'm sorry, Bloom." She didn't say anything.

This was going really badly. "Look, I just wanted to see what it would feel like. To be a regular guy for once."

"Yeah, well, I understand all of that," Bloom replied. "But you didn't have to lie to me and humiliate me."

Sky winced then hung his head. "I didn't mean to hurt you," he said. He looked into her eyes. "I care about you, Bloom. That's why I'm breaking off my arranged marriage to Diaspro."

"I'm so glad!" Bloom bit her lower lip. "I mean . . . it's cool you are, because you know, arranged marriages are, like, so old school."

"I feel terrible," said Sky. "Is there anything I can do to make it up to you?"

"Actually, there is one thing," Bloom replied.

Sky caught his breath. "Okay," he said.

"It's too weird to call you Prince Sky," said Bloom. "So, I want to call you something else."

"Sure, whatever you want," he replied eagerly.

Bloom gave a sly smile. "How about, uh . . . baby?"

Sky felt as if a ten-ton weight was just pulled off of his chest. "That's cool!" he said. They both burst into laughter.

CHAPTER 14

Bloom thought the short flight back to Alfea was a nice break. Unfortunately, it didn't last long enough. As soon as the ship landed, Miss Faragonda and Professor Saladin were there to greet them. Bloom wasn't looking forward to coming back empty-handed.

"Welcome home, girls," said Faragonda. "I'm glad you're all safe."

"Thanks, Miss Faragonda," said Bloom.

With his hands clasped behind his back, Professor Saladin approached the boys. "So, were you able to help the girls?" He wore a pleasant smile.

"Actually, they were fine without us," replied Sky.

Saladin's smile vanished. "So, you broke formation, risked your lives *and* one of my ships for nothing?"

"He's just being modest," Bloom interrupted. She wanted the boys to look good in front of their headmaster. "They totally saved us back there!"

Stella caught on immediately. "Yes, they should definitely get major extra credit!"

Saladin huffed, and then gave a knowing smirk.

As they walked toward the main hall, Bloom told Miss Faragonda about what happened on Sparks. She saw the disappointment in the woman's eyes when she found out that Bloom didn't retrieve the Dragon Fire.

"Check it out," Musa interrupted. She pointed to Kiko playing beside a large hedge. "Kiko made a new friend!" The little bunny was playing with a black duckling.

"How weird," said Stella. "That's Icy's duck, Pepe! How did he get here?"

Just then, Knut stepped out from behind the hedge. "Uh, I brought him with me."

"Trouble!" Stella took a step back.

"It's alright," Faragonda assured. "The ogre is on our side now."

"He helped in the fight against the witches, so we're letting him stay," Saladin explained.

"That's peachy with me, as long as he improves his hygiene," Stella joked.

Knut scratched his head. "I'm sorry if I'm a little stinkier than usual. I had to do a lot of fighting." Everyone laughed while Knut scratched his head. "What?"

Miss Faragonda stopped laughing and held up a hand. "Young ladies, the situation has become extremely dire. In my entire career I've never had to deal with anything like this."

Saladin smiled. "Once you get settled in, we'll sit down and discuss the best course of action."

"We need to be prepared for the worst now," said Faragonda. "They will surely try to destroy Alfea next."

Sky and the others didn't settle in at all. They immediately began to help the other Red Fountain students prepare their weapons and ready themselves for the next attack. It turned out that the heroes from Red Fountain and the fairies from Alfea made a great team. They quickly turned Alfea into quite a fortress. Sky just hoped it was enough to stop the witches' army.

Before long, Sky and Brandon were summoned to Miss Faragonda's office. When they got there, the door was already open. Faragonda and Saladin were joined by Bloom, Stella, and Knut.

The headmistress had a hand on Bloom's shoulder. "Bloom, I must ask you one more time. Are you absolutely sure you want to do this?"

"I know it's dangerous, but I don't have any other choice," Bloom replied. "It's what I have to do."

"Excuse me," Sky interrupted. "What do you have to do?"

Saladin turned to the two boys. "We're sending you on a mission to infiltrate Cloud Tower."

"What?" asked Brandon.

"Bloom, how can you think of going anywhere near the witches when you don't even have your powers?" asked Sky.

"Listen, I have to believe that I'll get the Dragon Fire back," Bloom replied. "I don't know how, but I do know this is the right course."

"How will we get in?" Brandon asked.

"We'll take the tunnels," Knut answered. "When I was a little ogre, I used to play in the tunnels, so I know my way around down there."

"Once we get in, we'll figure the rest out, okay?" said Bloom.

Sky wasn't only frightened for Bloom's safety; he was concerned about the lack of strategy. "You're disregarding the first lesson of tactics. You always need to have a plan."

"Except that there is no way to have a plan," Bloom explained. "The way I see it, we can either stay here and be totally overwhelmed, or we can do something." She smiled. "So what do you guys say? Are you with me?"

Sky returned the smile. "Of course we're with you."

"Bloom, I want you to proceed with caution, but also with haste," said Faragonda. She turned and looked at the darkening sky. "The signs are unmistakable. The final attack is coming."

CHAPTER 15

With only a torch lighting the way, Knut led them through the secret tunnel from Alfea to Cloud Tower. With sword at the ready, Sky followed behind him. Bloom was next, followed by Stella and Brandon.

They tromped through mud and a musty smell filled the air. Snakes slithered away and spiders crawled into their webs as the group passed. Bloom tried to be brave. No matter what they ran into, she would have to face it without magic. Eventually, she would have to confront the witches themselves. Bloom glanced around and tried to make the best of the situation. She supposed the dank tunnel *could* be an interesting place — if you were a young ogre.

Behind her, someone else was trying to be brave as well.

"So, Stella," Brandon began. "If we survive, do you want to catch a movie sometime?"

"Are you sure you're not a prince?" asked Stella.

"Yeah, definitely," Brandon replied. "I'm just an average squire."

Stella sighed. "Honestly, I've never dated a nonprince before."

"I guess that means you don't want to go out with me," said Brandon. He sounded very disappointed.

"I didn't say that," Stella teased. "It simply means that we have to take it one step at a time, like we could *start* with the movie!"

As they neared Cloud Tower, the tunnel widened. Neat stones began to line the walls instead of dangling roots and dirt. They passed several forks, but Knut assured them he knew where they were going. "I'm following the smell of a donut I left in the dorms a few days ago," he said. "Ogres have an excellent sense of smell."

After a few more feet, Knut stopped. Bloom was about to ask why when she heard a distant scratching sound.

"What's that?" asked Stella.

"Yeah, I hear it too," said Bloom.

The sound grew louder. Knut took a step forward. He held out the torch to light the corridor.

All of a sudden, the passage before them became covered in insects. The slimy bugs crawled over the floor, walls, and ceiling, and began skittering toward Bloom and the others.

Sky grabbed Bloom's hand. "Tactical retreat!" he shouted

as he yanked her away from danger. With his blazing sword leading the way, Sky led them back the way they came. When they reached one of the splits in the tunnel, they took it.

The sound of the insects faded. "I think we're losing them," Bloom said. She felt as if things were going well for once. Then the ground gave way under her feet.

The group yelled as they slid down a long and winding chute. They tumbled over each other as they picked up speed. A pungent stench filled the air as they were finally spit out into the open. They toppled onto a soft pile of full trash bags.

"Nice," Bloom said as she got to her feet. "We end up in the garbage dump!"

They found themselves just outside Cloud Tower. Steam rose from the surrounding muck and flies buzzed around the putrid piles of refuse.

Sky looked up at the dark towers. "At least we're almost there."

Brandon helped Stella to her feet. "There's probably a service entrance somewhere," he said.

"This better not rub off on my clothes," Stella said as she pinched her nose. "With the current situation, it'll be impossible to find a dry cleaner that's open."

Bloom smiled. "Don't you have twelve of the same outfit?" She grabbed one of Knut's arms and helped him to his feet. "Come on."

The ground bubbled around their feet. "What is that smell?" asked Sky.

Stella waved a hand in front of her face. "Yeah, it just got way stinkier in here!"

The muddy soil churned, and then exploded around them. Giant creatures burst from the muck.

"Beetle roaches!" yelled Knut.

Five of the huge insects encircled the small group. Each of the insects had eight hairy legs and a body the size of a minivan. They had tiny heads with crimson eyes and wide mouths filled with sharp teeth.

"I think I might puke," said Stella.

"They'd like that," said Knut.

Brandon activated his energy spear. "Be ready to pinch your nose," he said. "I think these release a thirty-mile-wide stench when destroyed."

Bloom grabbed his arm. "Wait! If we destroy them, the witches will smell them and know we're here."

"That's true," Sky agreed. "But it means we're going to have to come up with a way to make them leave us alone without having to burst them open."

The huge roaches creeped closer.

"Right! Let's stand here and negotiate with these giant bugs," said Stella. She turned to the closest roach. "If you leave, I'll give you all my trash for a month."

Suddenly, a hooded figure flew through the air and landed on the back of the biggest roach.

"Who's that?" asked Sky.

The giant beast leapt up and down like a bucking bronco. "Yee-ha!" yelled the mysterious figure. He reached into his tattered cloak and pulled out an energy pistol. "Get lost!" he yelled as he fired the pistol in front of the roach's face.

The giant bug roared and skittered away. The hooded figure leapt off its back, somersaulted in midair, and landed safely on the ground. The rest of the giant roaches followed the first one.

"How did he make the bugs leave?" asked Stella.

"That was the queen roach," said their mysterious savior. "The rest follow her."

"Hey, thanks," said Sky. "Whoever you are."

"Long time no see, buddy," the boy replied. He dropped his tattered cloak to reveal the flowing cape and blue and white jumpsuit that was the Red Fountain uniform.

"Riven!" Sky shouted.

"Where have you been all of this time?" asked Brandon.

Riven told them how he'd fallen for Darcy but then she had betrayed him at the end. The three witches cast him into a dark void that sent him straight to the dungeons below Cloud Tower.

"Miss Griffin and the other witches are locked down there, too," Riven explained. "With her help, I was able to pick the lock and escape."

"Maybe we should help them escape," Bloom suggested.

"They're all right," Riven assured her. "They were working on a major spell when I left."

"What happened next?" asked Brandon.

"After I escaped, I ran into a group of rot monsters," Riven explained. "I had no choice but to jump through one of the windows. Luckily, I remembered how to use my cape for aerodynamic gliding from Survival 101. Once on the ground, I used that tattered cloak to blend in. I was going to make my way out when I ran into you guys."

"I've known you since the first day of orientation." Brandon smiled. "And I've *never* seen you taking notes."

"No offense, but all this time I thought you were the Red Fountain slacker," said Sky.

Riven hung his head. "Listen, guys, I really hope you can forgive me for everything that has happened. I've been acting like a real jerk."

"Of course we forgive you." Sky slapped him on the back. "Anyone can fall for the wrong girl."

Bloom nudged Sky and smiled. "We're big on forgiveness these days."

"You coming with us?" asked Brandon.

Riven grinned. "You bet!"

As Bloom and the others climbed through a doorway into the castle, they didn't notice a large spider following them. The size of a large dog, the spider quietly skittered after them on eight hairy legs. It leapt into the corridor after them and climbed the wall. Silently, it scurried along the ceiling. It ran past the group and waited for them in a large chamber.

As the group emerged into the chamber, the spider opened the hard shell on its back. Its entire body was one big eyeball and the shell was its eyelid. The eye focused on Bloom and her friends.

CHAPTER 16

Icy stared into the back of the arachnacam. It magically networked with every other arachnacam in Cloud Tower. Darcy and Stormy gathered close as Bloom and the others walked into view.

"I'm glad you're here, Riven," said Sky. "We could really use the extra hand to take on those witches."

Icy chuckled. "They're going to need a lot more than an extra hand to take us on."

"Could they be any more naive?" asked Stormy. "They're making this so easy."

"While the Army of Decay is recharging, we can personally crush Bloom and Stella," said Darcy.

"Not to mention their loser Red Fountain groupies and that traitor ogre," Darcy added. "It'll be the perfect end to a perfect day!"

"All right, ladies," said Icy. "We need something really diabolic, yet fun at the same time."

"Let's freeze them first," said Darcy. "Then we'll crush them!"

Icy yawned dramatically. "Been there, done that."

"Whatever!" Darcy crossed her arms. Stormy tried to stifle a giggle.

Icy snapped her fingers. "I'll tell you what we'll do. We'll make Bloom think she can take the Dragon Fire back! We'll raise her hopes, she'll think it's hers, and then we'll snatch it out of her hands!"

Stormy nodded. "Nice."

"We'll make her cry," said Icy.

"We'll make her weep!" added Darcy.

"We'll make her wail!" said Stormy.

As Bloom followed Knut through the corridors of Cloud Tower, something strange happened. She felt a tickle in the pit of her stomach. Then it grew to be something more. It felt as if a tiny candle had been lit deep inside her. "Wait, guys. Stop!" she said.

"What is it?" asked Stella.

"I think . . ." She waited until she was sure. The feeling inside her felt warmer. "I think I sense the Dragon Fire. We're getting closer."

"Awesome," said Stella.

"We'll follow you, Bloom," said Sky.

Bloom took the lead as they proceeded down the long corridor. When they reached the end, they found themselves at the bottom of a wide staircase. The feeling grew stronger. Bloom broke into a run, taking the steps two at a time. The others ran after her. When they reached the top, they came to a pair of bloodred doors.

"The Dragon Fire!" Bloom pointed straight ahead. "It's behind those doors!"

"Are you sure?" asked Riven.

"Yes," Bloom replied. "I can sense its presence."

She cautiously pushed open the heavy doors and stepped though. She entered a round, empty room. Amber light danced off the bare walls — the light from the center of the room. The glow came from a small fire burning on a pedestal in the center of the chamber.

"Is that it?" asked Sky.

"Yeah!" Bloom replied. She moved toward the dancing flames. "The Dragon Fire! At last, I have it back." She reached toward the fire. "Now I'll be able to stop the witches." As her fingers neared the flames, it transformed into a jagged block of ice.

"I don't think so!" said a voice behind her. "Sorry, no Dragon Fire for you!"

Bloom turned to see Icy, Darcy, and Stormy standing at the front entrance. "You witches!" she yelled.

The Red Fountain boys activated their weapons, but it was too late. As if blowing a kiss, Icy blew toward the group. She sent them flying across the room. Everyone but Bloom slammed against the opposite wall and slid to the ground.

Bloom balled her hands into fists. "I'm going to get

the Dragon Fire back!" she shouted. "It's my destiny to have it!"

"That's not your destiny," Icy hissed. "Your destiny's to be locked in here for eternity! Because that's what losers get!"

"And you're the ultimate loser!" Stormy added.

"You're powerless and you're responsible for the destruction of an entire realm," Darcy sneered.

Stormy laughed. "You might be the biggest loser in history."

CHAPTER 17

Bloom was trapped. Sky, Stella, and the others slowly got to their feet at the other side of the chamber. They still seemed a bit groggy, though. It looked as if Bloom had to face the witches alone — and without any magic.

A green blast slammed into the witches from behind. They flew over Bloom's head and smashed into the wall next to her friends. Bloom saw a familiar silhouette in the doorway.

"Miss Griffin!" Bloom shouted. "That was so awesome!"

The headmistress strolled past Bloom. Her attention was on the three witches. "This is *my* school!" she barked.

Bloom's friends ran past Miss Griffin and joined Bloom by the doorway.

Icy slowly got to her feet. "We're not scared of you, Griffin," she growled. "We're not your students anymore. And we're more powerful than you'll ever be!"

Stormy put a hand to her head. "Then how can she knock us around like that?"

"Because you're a bunch of high school dropouts and I am the headmistress of Cloud Tower," Griffin answered. She turned to Bloom and the others. "I'll contain them while we go back to Alfea and regroup. Everybody prepare to leave."

Icy glared at the headmistress. "Oh yeah, you *better* run!"

Miss Griffin crossed her arms. "I know you'll get your power back and that you'll come after me. But when we meet again, I'll be ready for you." She pointed a bony finger at the three girls. "You have dishonored Cloud Tower and you will pay!"

Green light flashed from the woman's fingertip. The light expanded to create a giant force field, trapping the three witches.

"What is she doing?" asked Darcy. "It looks like some kind of advanced magic."

"What I'm doing is putting you in detention," Griffin answered. She turned and walked toward Bloom and the others. As she did, jagged stone spikes erupted from the floor and ceiling. The spikes overlapped in front of the witches, trapping them further. "And don't even think about leaving without a hall pass!" Griffin added.

Bloom and the others ran out of the room to find the Cloud Tower students waiting outside. They each wore long black robes and looked at the fairies with suspicion.

Miss Griffin stepped out of the room. "Let's go!" The doors slammed behind her. "The kind of power they have is tremendous. That spell won't contain them for long."

The headmistress led the way as the entire group climbed a long, spiraling staircase. "We're going to the terrace," she informed them. "We need to get to the highest elevation possible."

"Miss Griffin, what's going to happen once they break down the wall?" asked Bloom.

"I'm not sure," she replied. "But believe me, we don't want to be here to find out."

"So we're just going to leave?" asked Stella. "What about the Dragon Fire? We went through a lot so we could get in here and take it back."

"We do need to get it back," Griffin agreed. "And you fairies were very brave to come here by yourselves. You should certainly get plenty of extra credit for your efforts." She reached the top of the stairway and pushed open the doors to the terrace. She stood by the doorway as her students filed through. "But the truth is that you have no chance against them right now. I must combine my powers with Saladin and Faragonda. We stand for the three points of magic. Only then might we be able to take the power back."

Once everyone was assembled on the large terrace, Miss Griffin moved to the center. "I'll conjure up a Vorpal Tunnel to take us right to Alfea." She raised her hands toward the dark clouds above. Lightning flashed and the cold wind grew stronger. "You have to allow the energy of the portal to sweep you up," Griffin instructed. "It will not work if there's any resistance."

A shaft of green light pierced through the clouds. It shot down from the sky to form a large circle of light in the center of the terrace. "Enter the portal in alphabetical order," Griffin instructed. "Go!"

One by one, the witches stepped into the light. Then they gently floated up toward the sky.

Bloom heard a familiar sound behind them. Several rot monsters ran up a narrow exterior staircase. Their huge claws snapped with every step.

"The monsters are coming!" Bloom yelled.

"Everyone get in!" yelled Griffin. "Hurry!"

The young witches picked up the pace. Soon, the last of them floated up to the clouds. All that was left was Miss Griffin, Bloom, and her friends.

"What are you waiting for?" Griffin asked. "Hop in!"

"No," said Sky. "If the monsters get into the portal, there'll be no way to stop them!" He took a step forward. "I'll stay behind and guard your escape."

The headmistress aimed a bony finger toward the young prince. For a moment, Bloom thought she was going to zap him. Instead, a narrow beam of light shot from her fingertip and hit the ground in front of him. A levabike appeared. It was the sportiest model Bloom had ever seen.

"Here," said Griffin. "Use this to get to Alfea."

"Thanks!" said Sky.

He jumped on the bike and locked his feet in place. Once he did, metal bands appeared and began to wrap around his legs. The bands climbed higher until his entire body was covered in a special armor. A helmet with a narrow red visor appeared on his head.

He looked down at the armor. "Sweet!"

"Hold on," Bloom said as she climbed on behind him. "You're going to need help. I'm coming with you."

Sky smiled. "That's great! You and me together, well I can't think of a better battle team anywhere!"

More metal bands appeared until Bloom wore her own suit of armor and helmet.

Sky started the bike and turned it away from the portal. "Now, let's get those rot monsters out of here!"

"Good luck," said Riven as he stepped into the portal.

"See you back in Alfea," Stella yelled.

Bloom looked over her shoulder and watched her friends enter the portal. As she saw them rise into the clouds, she wondered if she would ever see them again.

CHAPTER 18

Sky revved the engine and spun the levabike in a circle. "Okay. Let's keep them away from the portal!"

The giant rot monsters poured onto the terrace and surrounded the shaft of light. However, all of their crimson eyes were on Sky and Bloom.

"I don't think it's the portal they're interested in," said Bloom.

"Hold on tight," said Sky. The bike zoomed toward the nearest beast.

"Okay, you drive and I'll swat," said Bloom.

Just before crashing into three of the rot monsters, Sky turned sharply. Bloom's leg shot out and kicked them off the terrace.

"Nice one!" shouted Sky.

They banked sharply, then drove toward another group. Sky and Bloom ducked in unison as a sharp claw snapped at their heads. This time, Sky slammed the front of the bike into one of the beast's heads. It spun around and slammed into two more of them.

Bloom looked over her shoulder and saw the end of the portal rise into the clouds. There was no way those monsters could get to it now. "The portal's gone," she said.

"Good, let's get out of here!" Sky turned the bike once more and pulled back the throttle. The levabike hummed loudly as it zoomed straight toward four of the beasts. "Hold on!" he yelled.

Bloom held tight to Sky's waist as they rammed into the monsters and shot off the edge of the terrace. Rot monsters briefly floated around them before falling to the ground. The levabike stayed in midair.

"I *totally* have to get one of these!" Sky yelled over the hum of the engine.

He pointed the bike downward and they flew toward the road below. The sun had set and it was hard to see, but he made it anyway. Sky accelerated as the bike settled to an altitude of just three feet.

"Are you sure we can go this fast?" asked Bloom.

Sky swerved to miss an attacking rot monster. "No, but I don't think we have much choice." He zigzagged through more of them. They were scattered all down the road.

Bloom saw movement from the corner of her eye. She looked down and saw several slimy insects crawling on her arm. "They're on me," she yelled. The repulsive bugs began to tear into her armor with their claws.

"I'll shake them off," Sky said. He tilted the bike left and right. "I don't know how much faster I can go. Just hold on, okay?" He hit the thrusters. It was all Bloom could *do* to hold on.

Bloom looked down at her arms and legs. She didn't see a bug anywhere. "All right! They're gone!"

As they came to a fork in the road, Sky veered left. "I'm going to take the forest road!" He released the throttle and the bike began to slow.

BOOM! Something rocked the bike. A bright flash filled Bloom's visor. "What was that?" she asked.

Sky swerved and accelerated. "We must have hit a defense system!" He turned just as another explosion jarred them. "Hold on!"

"Should we stop?" asked Bloom.

Sky released the throttle, but they continued to pick up speed. "The bike won't let me. It's not responding!"

Bloom looked back to see smoke billowing from a hole in the back of the bike.

"There's a hairpin turn coming up," Sky warned.

Bloom saw the sharp turn. A small guardrail separated them from a major drop-off. As they sped toward the curve in the road, it was clear that they weren't going to make it.

"Oh no!" Bloom yelled.

They blasted through the guardrail and shot out over the treetops. They held on tight as the bike spun out of control. They arced downward and ripped through the high branches of the forest below.

CHAPTER
19

Flora was worried about Bloom and Stella. She shouldn't have let them go to Cloud Tower alone. Sure, they were with Prince Sky and Brandon. But Bloom was still powerless.

She turned her attention back to her friends. They were all hanging out in her and Bloom's room. It was as if being there made them feel closer to Bloom somehow. Everyone was passing the time as well as they could. Once the students had prepared the school for the next attack, there wasn't much to do. Tecna and Timmy had created an early warning system. Musa had re-sorted her vast music collection — twice. Even Kiko was passing the time. He happily played with Icy's duck, Pepe. As for Flora, she was working on yet another counterspell to help Mirta.

Mirta was a young witch who had befriended Bloom. Mirta had even warned her about an attack planned by Icy, Darcy, and Stormy. For her kindness, the three witches turned her into a pumpkin. Now she stayed in Bloom and

Flora's room with the rest of Flora's enchanted plants. Ever since then, Flora had been working on a spell to change her back.

"Poor Mirta." Flora ran a hand across the large pumpkin. "I feel like I've done everything I can."

Musa put down a stack of CDs and joined her. "You might as well toss it in, Flo."

"You don't mean give up?" asked Flora.

"Look, if anyone of us could break Icy's spell, it's you," said Tecna. "And obviously, it's not working."

Flora sighed. "I don't want to give up on her."

"Then use all your Winx in one last try," Musa suggested. "We'll add our power to yours."

One of Mirta's vines reached out and coiled around Flora's wrist. "Look! It's as if Mirta agrees," said Tecna. "Let's go for it!"

The girls closed their eyes. Flora concentrated on Mirta. She could feel Musa and Tecna doing the same. Soon, through her mind's eye, she saw herself floating in a dark void. "Reach out for me, Mirta," she said.

"Something's happening!" said Musa.

Flora could feel it, too. Peering into the blackness, she could see a face deep in the void. It was a young face, with a cute nose and a few freckles. Soon, more of the girl came into view. Her short, red hair waved as if she was underwater.

"Flora!" Mirta said. She reached out a hand.

Flora reached toward her. "Mirta!" She concentrated on

the two of them touching. Their hands moved closer to one another. She could swear they touched just before . . . *BAM!*

Flora opened her eyes to see a cloud of white smoke. She looked down on the desk. Mirta was gone.

"Where'd she go?" asked Musa.

"Is she gone?" asked Tecna.

"I'm right here," said a voice behind them. They turned to see the young girl standing on the other side of the room. She looked completely normal. The only remnants of her former pumpkin self was the cartoon pumpkin printed on her T-shirt.

"Mirta!" said Flora. "I'm so glad to see you!"

"And I'm glad to have arms and legs again," Mirta joked. "Thanks for not giving up on me, Flora!"

Flora gave her a hug. "No problem!"

Musa picked up Kiko and Pepe. "Now, let's all go outside and enjoy the sunshine while we can."

The girls ran outside and sat on the cool grass in the courtyard. Nearby, Miss Faragonda was conferring with Professor Saladin and Master Codatorta.

"The Alfea girls and the Red Fountain boys are working well together," said the headmistress.

"Next year, we'll have to bring them together under happier circumstances," said Saladin.

"If there is a next year," Codatorta added. "This could be the end."

"Why can't you be more positive, like our students?"

asked Faragonda. "Why, just this morning, some of them organized a pep rally. They were saying things like, *We can do it* and *Bring it on*."

Codatorta sighed. "That's youth talking."

A sinking feeling in her stomach tore Flora from her eavesdropping. Over the years, she had become extremely in tune with her feelings and her surroundings. She knew exactly what this feeling meant. She leapt to her feet and ran toward the group of adults.

"Miss Faragonda!" she shouted. "Something's coming!" Musa, Tecna, and Mirta caught up with her. Flora pointed to a spot in the quad about twenty feet away. "I can sense a Vorpal Tunnel opening right over there!"

They watched as the air in the spot began to ripple.

"Is it a sneak attack?" asked Musa.

"Look!" yelled Tecna. "Something's materializing!"

The ripple began to solidify into a shape. Several shapes. A group of people appeared and walked toward them.

"It's Stella!" Flora shouted. "They're back!"

"And they rescued the imprisoned witches!" Musa added.

Miss Griffin appeared first, followed by Stella, Brandon, Riven, and Knut. Behind them, the entire student body of Cloud Tower slowly filed out of the tunnel.

Miss Faragonda stepped forward and met Miss Griffin. "How long has it been since you set foot on the Alfea campus?"

Miss Griffin smirked. "We were juniors. Ediltrude and

I were sneaking onto campus to turn the Ky-Fly sorority into goats."

"Aah, yes," Faragonda replied. "If memory serves me, I believe you left our campus seven inches tall . . . in a jar."

Griffin's smirk disappeared. It was replaced by a wide smile. "Those were happier times, weren't they?"

"With all of us banding together, perhaps those happier times can return," said Faragonda.

Flora, Mirta, Tecna, and Musa ran up to Stella and the others. "Where's Bloom?" asked Flora.

"We don't know what happened to her and Sky," Brandon replied. "They stayed behind to keep the monsters from entering the tunnel.

"They were supposed to meet us back here," Stella added.

"Oh, dear," said Flora. Now she was *really* worried.

CHAPTER 20

"Aaaaah!" Icy screamed as she blasted away the last of the imprisoning spikes. Darcy and Stormy had pooped out three layers ago. It had been up to Icy to break through the last of their detention cell. She couldn't believe that old witch had the power to imprison them like that.

"After we've had time to rest, Griffin is going to pay for that!" Icy barked as she marched out of the room.

"I can't believe those traitor witches are hanging with the pixies at Fairy High," said Darcy.

Stormy laughed. "Those idiot weaklings actually think they'll be safe cowering in the halls of Alfea."

"While we get our strength back, let's send them something to keep them busy," Darcy suggested.

"Good idea," said Icy. "We'll send a battalion to Cutesy Academy! That school is finally going to get the schooling it deserves!"

*   *   *

Bloom and Sky made their way through the dark woods. Their armor had protected them from the levabike crash. They were intact, but their bike wasn't. They had decided to walk to the city of Magix. Once there they could find a ride to Alfea.

"Would it be quicker to go through Black Mud Swamp?" asked Bloom.

"It would," Sky replied. "But these treetops will provide better cover for us."

"I guess you're right," Bloom said. She saw one of the witches' stingrays swoop through the clouds above. "Those winged monsters are probably patrolling the whole realm."

"Let's take a break," Sky said as he stopped beside a large boulder. He sat down, and then patted the rock beside him. Bloom joined him.

"Sky, I'm scared," she said.

"What's wrong?" asked Sky.

"Without my powers, I feel like the helpless little girl from Earth," Bloom explained.

"You're not, though. You're the last Princess of Sparks!" He put an arm around her. "That's pretty awesome."

Bloom rested her head on his shoulder. "I know, but the only thing separating some normal girl from Gardenia from the last Princess of Sparks was a magic power that I no longer have."

"When you learned the truth about me, you told me it didn't change who I was," explained Sky.

"Yeah, but that was you and . . ."

"Nothing can change who you are," Sky interrupted. "Some things can't be taken away."

Bloom sighed. She supposed he was right. Although she didn't feel like a princess. She felt more like a lost little girl.

Sky nudged her with his shoulder. "Come on. The quicker we get to Magix, the quicker we can find transportation to Alfea."

Bloom was about to stand when she heard a distant voice. *Lake Chrysalis,* the voice said. *Come to Lake Chrysalis.*

Bloom grabbed Sky's arm as he stood. "Hold up. Did you hear that?"

He looked around. "Hear what?"

"I thought I heard a voice just now," said Bloom.

"I didn't hear a thing," said Sky. "But these woods are full of creatures. Come on, let's get going."

Bloom could barely make out what the voice was saying. Was that Daphne's voice?

CHAPTER 21

Stella stood in the quad with the rest of the students. The fairies stood in rows down the center. The boys from Red Fountain stood on their right while the witches from Cloud Tower stood on the left. It felt weird having the students from all three schools at Alfea. Stella looked to her right and caught Brandon sneaking a glance at her. He quickly turned straight ahead. Then again, having temporary guests was kind of fun.

The teachers from all three schools stood on the landing in front of the main building. Miss Faragonda stepped forward. "You have all fought very bravely," she said. "But this is not over. Our true test is yet to come." As the headmistress paused, whispers escaped the gathered students. They quickly hushed as she resumed her speech. "Fairies, witches, and heroes, dig down deep and muster all your magic and power."

Miss Griffin stepped forward. "If we all work together, I know that we can triumph!"

Professor Saladin joined them. "According to Timmy and Tecna's detection device, another attack wave is on the way. It's the biggest one yet." He raised his staff over his head. "Now, when we give the signal, everyone . . ."

"Here they come!" yelled a distant voice.

They turned to see one of the Red Fountain boys on the east wall. He pointed toward the hundreds of flying stingrays in the sky. There were so many that they seemed more like an approaching storm than an approaching attack force.

"You have to be kidding!" said Stella. "There's, like, thousands of them!"

"Everyone to your positions!" ordered Faragonda.

Immediately, everyone broke formation and dashed to their assigned posts. Some ran, some flew, but everyone got there as fast as he or she could.

"Look at the sky!" Bloom shouted. She pointed to the thousands of stingrays flying overhead. "They're headed straight for Alfea!"

Sky picked up the pace. "We have to get to Magix immediately!"

Bloom hurried after him. Then she heard the voice again. She stopped to listen. It was much clearer now.

Find me, Bloom! the voice said. It was a lady's voice. It was Daphne! *Come to Lake Chrysalis.*

Sky stopped and turned around. "What's wrong?"

"Okay, don't tell me you didn't hear that," said Bloom.

"Hear what?" asked Sky.

"It's Daphne. She's calling me!" Bloom held up a finger. "Listen . . ."

Bloom, Daphne called. *Come, Bloom!*

Sky shook his head. "I don't hear anything." He listened for a moment longer then shook his head again. "Come on, we have to get moving."

"No, you go on ahead," Bloom said. "I have to go to Lake Chrysalis right now."

"What are you talking about?" asked Sky.

"This voice I've been hearing, maybe it's not even Daphne, maybe it's just a voice inside of me," she explained. "Either way, I have to listen to it. I have to go."

Sky walked toward her. "Fine, then I'm coming with you!"

Bloom put out a hand. "No, Sky, I have to do this alone. Please understand."

Sky looked as if he was about to object. Instead, he merely sighed. "All right," he said. "Just meet me in Magix in two hours. If you're not there, I'm coming to find you. Okay?"

"Okay," Bloom replied. She gave him one last smile before turning and hiking into the woods — alone.

CHAPTER 22

Stella spun her scepter, and then blasted two more of the flying stingrays. Behind her, Tecna, Musa, and Flora shot down stingrays of their own. They stood with their backs to one another as they countered the monster's version of a vile air strike.

Bright beams of colorful light erupted all over Alfea. As long as the sky was thick with flying beasts, most of the fairies remained on the ground. Along with the witches, they blasted the enemy overhead. The heroes from Red Fountain manned the walls and the main gate. Their job was to fight off the approaching rot monsters and berserkers.

With her full attention on the sky, Stella almost missed the mass of bugs erupting from the ground in front of her. The squirming mound grew and transformed into one of the headless berserkers. It raised a giant fist, preparing to squash the group of fairies.

Stella looked up just in time. *"Relocatus!"* she yelled.

The fairies disappeared. The monster's fist slammed into the ground where they had just stood. They materialized just behind the bumbling beast.

Flora's hands glowed brightly.

"Do it, Flo!" Musa cheered.

A shaft of green light exploded from her hands. It blasted the creature in the back. A long vine appeared and coiled around the giant. He fell to the ground.

Another beast rose beside him. "Uh-oh, looks like he's got a friend," Stella warned.

Tecna and Musa rose into the air and hovered over the new attacker. Both blasted the beast with bolts of energy. It exploded into a million tiny insects. This time, however, the insects didn't squirm into the ground. The slimy bugs divided themselves into four piles. They scrambled over each other as they formed *four* rot monsters.

"They multiply exponentially," said Tecna.

Flora's bound giant quickly disintegrated into a heap of insects. They easily crawled out of the vines and formed a new mound. A new berserker rose from the churning mass. It raised its fists over where its head should have been.

"Hey, big guy, that is not slick or buff," Stella joked. "Just gross!"

A green blade split the beast in two. It disintegrated, revealing Brandon and Riven on the other side. "Hope you weren't talking about us!" Brandon said with a smile. "Let's show these things what's up!"

As the boys joined the battle, more monsters began to

rise from the ground. Brandon carved up another only to face two more. "Aw, come on!" he yelled.

"Hey, remember that move from Double Duel class?" asked Riven.

Brandon planted his sword into the ground. "I sure do, Riven!" He pulled a new weapon off his belt and activated it. A scarlet blade shot out from each side of the grip. "I'll lead, you follow!"

Brandon leapt onto the back of a nearby rot monster. The creature's flailing tentacles slurped the air wildly as it reached toward him. Brandon spun the double blades, and then pushed off. As he performed a backward somersault, Riven kicked the beast in the chest. It fell apart in four large pieces.

"That ought to keep him down!" said Riven.

Brandon pointed to pile of squirming bugs. They re-formed into the disgusting rot monster. "Then why's it getting up?"

Stella aimed her scepter and blasted the beast. It disintegrated into a million tiny pieces. This time, it didn't get back up. "We have to work together to defeat them," she said.

As the fairies, witches, and heroes began to combine their attacks, the creatures went down and stayed down. The enemy forces were beginning to thin, but there were still a lot of them to contend with.

A giant stingray swooped past Stella, nearly knocking

her off her feet. It grabbed Tecna in its claws and soared high above the school.

"Tecna!" yelled Stella.

"You want to get into it with me?" asked Tecna. She transformed her small neon fairy wings to the large wedge-shaped glider wings. "Take that!" she shouted as her wings tore through the flying beast.

"Someone do something about the rest of those flying stingrays!" yelled Brandon.

"I'm on it!" said a voice behind them. Stella turned and saw Timmy pointing his pistol toward the sky. "A couple of zaps from my B-kicker Blaster ought to do the trick!"

He fired his weapon at the swooping monsters. Stella and Musa joined in as well. Soon, the sky was once again filled with colorful beams of light. The few stingrays that were left flew away from the school.

The berserkers and rot monsters were thinning out as well. It looked as if they were winning.

Just then, an orange dome appeared over Alfea. Stella saw Miss Faragonda and Miss Griffin standing in the middle of the quad. Both had their arms raised as they each projected an orange beam of light toward the sky. They were feeding the dome.

"Fairies of Alfea, this is our moment!" yelled Faragonda. "Focus your energy into one attack!"

"Witches of Cloud Tower!" shouted Griffin. "Unite your powers with the fairies!"

"Now, girls!" Faragonda ordered.

"All of you!" Griffin added.

Stella closed her eyes and concentrated. She felt the burning power of Solaria rush out of her body to join the dome of energy. She could also feel everyone else's power combining with hers. It was amazing.

Through her mind's eye, she saw the orange glow envelope all of Alfea. The attacking beasts roared in defiance as they began to crumble. "It's working!" she shouted. "Keep it up, everybody!"

Soon, every disgusting monster had vanished. The students opened their eyes and began to cheer.

"They're gone!" shouted Flora.

"They're so totally gone!" Stella added. "Woo-hoo!"

Icy roared with fury. "Those losers actually defeated that wave of attacks?" The three witches crowded around the arachnacam. A tiny projection of the battlefield appeared inside the spider's large eye. Icy watched in disgust as the fairies, witches, and heroes cheered.

"How dare they?" asked Stormy.

"Look at them," Darcy huffed. "They probably think they've won."

"As if!" said Stormy.

"I'm sick of this game!" Icy slammed a fist onto the image below. "It's not fun anymore!" The arachnacam squealed in pain. It shut its eye and scurried out of the room.

Stormy crossed her arms. "We have to stop sitting back and just watching!"

"Seriously," Darcy agreed. "It's time to get our hands dirty. Let's get in there and bust out the full power of the Dragon Fire!"

Icy smiled. "Get your fighting boots on, girls. We're riding into battle!" She blew into her open palm. A small ice sculpture appeared. It looked like a tiny version of Alfea. Icy slowly began to close her fingers around the tiny model. "The walls of Alfea will crumble between our fingers! And we won't stop fighting until every pixie and traitorous witch is wiped off the face of the realm!" The tiny sculpture disintegrated.

CHAPTER 23

As Sky walked down the streets of downtown Magix, he couldn't believe his eyes. It was completely deserted. No witches, warlocks, or fairies walked the sidewalks. No leva-cars or leva-buses zoomed down the streets. And no lights were on in any of the spiraling buildings.

What's going on here? he asked himself. *Where is everybody?*

He turned corner after corner and saw more of the same. It was as if the city of Magix had been deserted for thousands of years.

Sky cupped his hands around his mouth. "Is anybody here?" His voice echoed off of the empty buildings. "If you're hiding, I'm one of the good guys!"

Sky walked into a coffee shop and was shocked at what he found there. Several people sat at the tables, unmoving. Their entire bodies were covered in some kind of webbed cocoons. It was as if a spider had trapped them.

"What have those witches done to these people?" Sky asked.

He moved closer to one of the webbed victims. It was difficult to tell, but it looked like a man. Sky put a hand to the man's neck. He felt a faint pulse. The man's chest slowly moved up and down.

At least they're still alive, Sky thought.

He stepped back outside. Maybe someone had survived the attack. He turned down another street. "Hello?" he asked.

Something clanked down a nearby alley. Sky turned back and looked around the corner. "Who's there?"

Just then, a dark shadow fell over him. He leapt out of the way just as a jagged claw slammed into the concrete. He activated his sword and turned to face the slimy rot monster.

"Come on!" Sky taunted. "I'm not afraid of a little slug!"

The monster reared its head back. Its many tentacles gyrated wildly. It was as if it were laughing. Several slime bugs emerged from the cracks in the street. They poured into the rot monster's feet and the beast doubled in size.

"Uh-oh," said Sky. "I had to say *little*."

CHAPTER 24

Bloom pushed aside a branch and found what she was searching for. The crystal waters of Lake Chrysalis stretched out before her. She gently stepped to the water's edge. It looked very peaceful and serene.

"Are you here, Daphne?" asked Bloom. "Were you calling for me?"

Bloom reached a foot toward the water's edge. As she did, the magical armor began to disappear. It unclasped itself in little strips all the way up her body. Soon, she was clothed only in her jeans and shirt.

She stepped into the cool water. "You're here, aren't you, Daphne? I can feel it."

Yes, Bloom, Daphne replied in her melodious voice. *I'm here.*

"How did you get here?" Bloom asked.

You brought me, Bloom, she replied.

"What?" she asked. "When did I do that?"

Come into the water, Daphne instructed. *So you can see me.*

Bloom took another step then stopped. "Okay, but there's a small problem. I can't really breathe under water."

Close your eyes, Bloom, said Daphne. *Picture yourself below the surface and you will be here. Believe and it will happen. It's time for you to find me, Bloom. It's time for you to complete your journey. Are you ready?*

"Yes, I'm ready." She took another step. The water was up to her knees now.

Come beneath the water. Leave the world behind and dive into yourself.

Bloom was a little frightened, but she trusted Daphne. She closed her eyes and pictured herself beneath the rippling surface. Bloom felt the water rise up her legs, past her waist, and over her face. As the cool liquid caressed her, she opened her eyes. She was under the water. She took a deep breath and felt air fill her lungs. The water was only an illusion.

"Whoa," Bloom said. "This is like when Miss Faragonda astral projected me."

Do you understand, now, Bloom? Daphne asked. *When Miss Faragonda projected you, all she did was take you deep into yourself. Not to a lake on another planet. You see, that's where I exist, Bloom, inside of you.*

Bloom found herself standing in front of a large underwater cave. "This is like some kind of dream." She stepped into the cave to see Daphne standing before her. She looked more beautiful than ever. Her gown swayed in the water and her golden glow was rippled through the liquid.

"A dream and a reality — together," said Daphne. "You're very close to finding your powers, Bloom. Keep looking."

Suddenly, a vision appeared to Bloom. She saw herself eating dinner with her parents.

"What do you see?" asked Daphne.

Bloom smiled. "I see my parents' house on Earth."

"That is the place you went after the coven destroyed the kingdom of Sparks," Daphne explained. "The place I took you to begin your journey. The place where you would grow up loved and unharmed until the time was right."

The vision changed. Bloom saw the three witches attacking Sparks. She saw Daphne place Bloom in the portal when Bloom was just a baby. She even saw her father pull her out of that burning building. He tipped back his fireman's helmet and stroked her short, red hair.

"Earth was wonderful," Daphne continued. "You had parents, friends, even people who didn't understand you."

The vision dissolved to Bloom as a young girl playing with her parents. Then she saw herself as teenager playing with Kiko. She even saw Trixy, the girl who lived on the same block and always gave Bloom a hard time.

"All of these things helped make you who you are," Daphne explained.

The vision morphed again. She relived the first time she met Stella. She saw herself entering Alfea.

"But who am I?" asked Bloom. "Earth girl or Princess of Sparks?"

"We are the sum of *all* our experiences," Daphne replied.

"The friends we make, the people we love. *All* of these things make us who we are. Ordinary Earth girl and heir to the royal Kingdom of Sparks."

Bloom saw herself laughing with her friends in their dorm. She saw herself battling the witches. She saw herself walking along the now frozen planet of Sparks. She saw herself come full circle, back to where she started.

"That is who you are," said Daphne. "Daughter of Mike and Vanessa and keeper of the Dragon Fire." Daphne faded away but her voice grew louder and echoed inside Bloom's head. *It can never be taken away from you. It's what's in your heart. Your journey is over. You have arrived!*

"Daphne?" Bloom was alone in the dark cave.

She walked out and looked at the rippling water above. "Who am I?" she asked herself. "What's inside me? What's inside my heart?"

Bloom felt something inside her all right — something burning. The flame grew until her entire body seemed to radiate. Tiny bubbles encircled her as the water around her began to boil.

"I am Bloom!"

Fire washed over her body.

"I am a princess!"

Wings sprouted from her back.

"I am the keeper of the Dragon Fire!"

Bloom blasted through the surface of the lake. She soared high above the clouds, a fairy once more.

"And no one will take that away from me!"

CHAPTER 25

Sky roared as he ran toward the giant rot monster. The huge beast opened one of its claws, ready to take off the hero's head. Sky ducked under the claw, spun around, and hacked it off with his sword. "How do you like me, now?" he asked.

The monster turned and held up its stump. Already, more insects crawled over it, forming a new claw.

"Great," said Sky. He backed away as the beast stomped forward. "Can't we just talk about this?"

Sky's back hit something hard. He turned to see that it was a giant berserker. He ducked as the goliath took a swing at him. He raised his sword and backed away from both of the disgusting creatures. Then he heard a familiar sound over his shoulder.

Tik-a-tik-a-tik-a-tik-a-tik-a-tik-a-tik-a-tik-a-tik-a . . .

Behind him, thousands of insects crawled up a tall building. They formed two more rot monsters. The creatures leapt from the wall and landed behind Sky. Now that they had him surrounded, they slowly moved in.

"Look, guys, I didn't mean to crash your party." He spun around, trying to keep an eye on all of them. "You probably just want to rot out. Maybe watch each other decompose or something."

Sky knew he didn't have a chance. They never taught him anything at Red Fountain that prepared him for this kind of attack. Maybe that would have been next year. He certainly didn't think they would have known how to fight this particular kind of enemy. Either way, he wasn't going down without courage and honor.

"Fine, then!" he yelled defiantly. "If that's what you want . . ." He waved his sword. "Bring it on!"

Just then, he heard the sweetest sound in all the realms.

"Hey there, tentacle-mouth!" Bloom yelled from above. "Back away from the prince!"

Sky looked up to see Bloom in full fairy attire. Her wings fluttered wildly as she hovered over them. "Am I glad to see you!" he shouted.

"Back at you, Sky," she replied. "Now hang on, I'm going to get you out of there!" A fireball appeared in Bloom's hand. She slammed it into the mega rot monster. The beast roared as he dissolved on the spot. "Nobody messes with my boyfriend!" Bloom shouted.

Sky didn't mind having a girl save his hide. Especially when it was someone like . . . *Did she just say "boyfriend"?*

Bloom sent another fireball sailing toward the berserker. Sky ducked as it exploded. Rotting bits flew everywhere. The other two rot monsters charged. They were dispatched with balls of fire as well.

Bloom landed beside Sky. "Sorry I was late," she said. "You okay?"

"Yeah," he replied, and then deactivated his sword. "But if you hadn't come along, I'd be worm food." He reached out and held her hand.

"Come on, that's not true," said Bloom.

Sky scratched his head. "So, uh, what was that about *nobody messes with my boyfriend,* did I hear you right?"

Bloom bit her lower lip. "I just needed something to shout." She looked away. "Like trash-talking in the heat of battle."

Now Sky looked away. "Yeah, I figured that's what it was." He looked down and saw that he still held her hand. A bit embarrassed, he let go and changed the subject. "So, your powers are back."

"They never left me," said Bloom. "I just hope I didn't realize that too late."

Sky smiled. "Better late than never."

Bloom looked around the deserted city. "So what happened here?"

"I'm not sure," replied Sky. "But I think the rot monsters did it with their tentacles. It seems the witches made them more powerful than last time."

Bloom walked over to a cocooned person on the

sidewalk. "Can these people be revived?" She knelt down and ran a hand over the webbing.

Sky knelt beside her. "I don't know."

Bloom leapt to her feet. "Stella! The girls! If those witches . . ."

"Let's not jump to any conclusions," Sky interrupted. "Let's just get back to Alfea."

"Leave that to me!" She held out a hand. "Grab on!"

CHAPTER 26

"**So you're a** witch, Mirta," said Flora. "Do you know any inside secrets on how we can defeat Icy, Stormy, and Darcy?"

Mirta shook her head. "They're on a whole different level. They're totally dedicated to destruction."

Stella and her friends sat on the main hall steps. As they waited for another attack, everyone seemed *way* too depressed.

"Maybe a manicure-pedicure combo would chill them out!" Stella joked.

Tecna crossed her arms. "Why are you turning this into a joke?"

"I'm just trying to lighten things up," Stella replied. She looked at her moping friends. "Although it doesn't look as if it's working."

"Hey, we're *all* worried about Bloom," said Flora. "But she's going to be fine."

"No way, no how is any rot monster or witch going to take down my girl Bloom," Musa agreed.

"I hope you're right, for all our sakes," said a voice behind them. Stella turned and saw Miss Faragonda and Miss Griffin.

Griffin turned to Faragonda. "Do you honestly think she's coming back?"

"Fairies don't give up on each other," Faragonda snapped. "I've always believed that Bloom is our only hope."

"And now?" asked Griffin. "Do you think there's another way we can win?"

"I have to believe there is, Griffin," Faragonda replied. "I need to believe, even if it's naive, that we are all capable of making a difference in our fate."

Miss Griffin smirked. "Spoken like a true pixie."

Suddenly, a horn sounded at the main gate. "They're coming!" shouted a Red Fountain boy. "And Icy, Darcy, and Stormy are with them!"

"So they've come to defeat us personally," said Griffin.

Miss Faragonda cupped her hands around her mouth. "Fairies, witches, and heroes, as we face our final battle, I want you to find all of your courage and all of your strength and turn all its power on Icy, Darcy, and Stormy!"

Griffin joined in. "If we have any hope for survival, those three must be defeated!"

"This is it!" shouted Faragonda. "Everybody, to your positions!"

CHAPTER 27

Icy, Darcy, and Stormy rode on tall thrones as they approached Alfea. Long columns of giant berserkers marched ahead of them. More columns of rot monsters brought up the rear. Above them, the sky was thick with slimy stingrays.

As the pixie school came into view, Icy could just make out all the pathetic fairies and witches flying around, trying to get ready.

"Stormy, when we're done, I'll put you in charge of what's *left* of Alfea," Icy said. "All the fairies will report to you."

Stormy laughed. "We'll have to do some remodeling. My throne won't fit in Faragonda's office. Know what I mean?"

"Sure do," Icy replied.

"Hey, Ice," said Darcy. "What about me?"

"You'll be in charge of Red Fountain," said Icy.

A thin smile stretched across Darcy's face. "That's cool."

"It's showtime, ladies!" said Icy. She leaned forward in her throne. "Attack!"

The first wave of berserkers charged the gate at full speed. They plowed through flashes of light and energy beams. The hulks who made it through the barrage slammed into the main wall of Alfea. Red Fountain boys leapt to the ground as the wall beneath them crumbled.

"Now we have a clear path into Alfea," said Icy. All that stood in their way now were a few columns of fairies, witches, and heroes. "This should thin their ranks!" With a flick of her wrist, Icy motioned the stingrays to attack. They swooped down toward the defenders.

Griffin and Faragonda raised their hands above their heads. "*Globus Shield!*" they yelled. Energy beams shot from their palms and formed a green dome over Alfea. The attacking stingrays slammed into the shield and vanished.

Stormy growled. "You can't stop me! I'm the new headmistress of Alfea!" She blasted the dome with an energy blast of her own. The green shield flickered once and then vanished. "Make room, fairies! We're moving in!"

"No way!" shouted Musa. "You're *so* not going to crash our crib!" The fairy shot a red ball of light toward Stormy.

The witch snatched the ball out of the air and examined it. "What's this? A joke?" She flicked it away with two fingers. "How pathetic."

Icy laughed. "Having the Dragon Fire so rules!" she said. "Doesn't it, ladies?"

"That's not the Dragon Fire!" yelled a voice from above.

Icy looked up to see something that chilled her already frigid veins. She saw Bloom hovering above them. She was dressed as a full-blown fairy. As her wings fluttered, she glowed bright orange. The ghostly image of a large dragon encircled her.

"This is the Dragon Fire!" Bloom shouted.

CHAPTER 28

Bloom looked down at her friends below. She was glad that she wasn't too late. But she was also worried that they would be upset with her for not arriving sooner.

"Sorry it took so long to get here," she yelled.

"No prob, Bloom!" yelled Musa.

"Go kick some witch booty!" shouted Stella. She turned to one of the nearby Cloud Tower students. "No offense."

Icy stood on her throne and growled with fury. "She has the Dragon Fire, too?! That's not fair!"

Bloom pointed at the evil witch. "You think you can invade my school, mess with my friends, and get away with it?" She formed a large ball of fire between her hands. With all her might, she threw it toward Icy. "*As if,* witches!"

Rot monsters scattered as the top of Icy's throne exploded. The defenders in Alfea cheered.

"Stormy, Darcy, get over here!" Icy said from above. She had slipped away at the last second. She hovered above the battlefield. "Give me your share of the Dragon Fire. I need it to take care of this uppity pixie!"

Darcy and Stormy flew from their thrones and joined Icy. Immediately, Stella, Flora, Musa, and Tecna took to the sky. They joined Bloom as she faced off against the witches.

Icy pointed to the fairies. "Don't worry. You won't need more than your regular powers to take on those four posers." She glared at Bloom. "As for you, Bloom, I'm going to show you just what a loser you are."

Icy held out a hand and blasted the fairies with a concentrated snowstorm. Bloom winced as ice struck her cheeks, but she didn't run. Instead, she concentrated and a large ball of fire appeared around her and her friends. Bloom focused and the ball expanded. It slammed into the three witches and sent them tumbling through the air.

Bloom soared straight for Icy. She zipped past the still recovering Darcy and Stormy. Icy's eyes widened as she flew away.

"We'll see who the loser is!" shouted Bloom.

She chased Icy all the way back to Lake Chrysalis. Icy skimmed across the water, turned, and fired ice missiles at Bloom. The fairy easily dodged them and shot back a blast of fire. Icy barely got out of the way. The water exploded behind her.

The witch flew high into the clouds, and then turned to face Bloom. She spun like a top as another of Bloom's fire blasts hit her. Bloom launched more fireballs, trying to keep her off balance. Twisting and turning, the witch dodged them. She spun and sent an icy blast toward Bloom. The fairy erected a fire shield just in time.

"I'm going to finish what the coven started!" Icy yelled. "They destroyed your precious little planet and I'll destroy you!"

Bloom growled with anger. She could hear the roar of the Dragon Fire as she turned it loose on Icy. The dragon's smoky image flew toward Icy. The evil witch held up a hand and the dragon froze. It turned to ice and crumbled away.

"I'm glad you got more Dragon Fire, Bloom," Icy sneered. "Because now there's more for me to steal!"

"You're not taking anything!" Bloom yelled. "The Dragon Fire is mine!"

CHAPTER 29

Stella was elated. Her best friend was safe. Better yet, Bloom had her powers back. And to top it off, while Bloom handled Icy, Stella and the others could take care of Darcy and Stormy once and for all.

While the two witches were distracted watching Icy and Bloom, Musa sent a red energy ball toward them. It slammed into the witches, sending them tumbling backward.

"You still think *that* was pathetic, Stormy?" asked Musa.

Darcy turned to Stormy. "Let's join our powers." The two witches held out their hands. "*Electric Twister!*" they yelled in unison.

A black tornado appeared before them. Electricity danced around it as it headed straight toward the fairies.

"*World Wide Web!*" shouted Tecna. She closed her eyes and a round cage appeared around her and her friends. It was just like the one they used on the snow giant. However, this one didn't trap them, it protected them from the spinning cyclone. As the twister hit, lightning bounced off of the cage and merely pushed them backward. The cage glowed brightly, and then exploded around them. Both the web and the twister were gone.

"Good one, Tec!" said Musa.

Stella didn't give the witches time to cast a new spell. She tightened her grip on her scepter. "*Sunburst!*" she yelled. A blast of light shot from the head of her scepter and slammed into Darcy and Stormy. The witches tumbled backward.

"*Ninja Daisies!*" shouted Flora. She created a spinning twister of her own. Hundreds of tiny daisies sprung from her palm and washed over the confused witches. Distracted, they still couldn't focus their power.

"Time to lay down some tracks, yo!" said Musa. With a flick of her wrist, two giant subwoofers appeared on either side of the witches. They clasped their hands to their ears as they were blasted by a funky hip-hop baseline.

"I'll shut it off," said Stormy. She reached for the clouds and lightning flashed around her. The electric bolts struck the speakers, blowing them to bits.

"Give it up, pixies," Darcy growled. "We're going to bury you next to Bloom!"

"No, you're not!" shouted Tecna.

The two witches floated closer. "I think this is the part where we relieve them of the burden of being irreparable dorks," said Darcy.

"Allow me," Stormy said as her eyes flashed. "I'll go crazy on them!" Electricity danced between her fingertips.

"*Psycho-Clone!*" The air around them flashed with lightning and an enormous cyclone appeared. Stella had never seen a tornado that big.

"Watch out," Tecna warned. "That funnel has an F-5 wind force!"

The fairies backed away as the tornado moved closer. Stella hit it with a blast from her scepter, but it didn't do any good. It actually seemed to make the cyclone stronger. Their fairy wings fluttered as they turned to get out of there. Flora wasn't fast enough. The tornado swallowed her and spun her around inside.

"It's got Flora!" yelled Stella.

"Flora!" they shouted. But their friend was helpless.

CHaPTER 30

Below, in Alfea, the fairies, witches, and heroes battled the biggest attack force ever. Brigades of heroes stood in the towers and blasted the flying stingrays. Fairies and witches flew over the battlefield below. They shot the berserkers and rot monsters with colorful energy bolts. Even more heroes fought off attacks with their energy weapons.

Prince Sky slashed through two rot monsters. He leapt into a flying somersault as a giant berserker swung at him. A sword sliced the beast up the middle and it disintegrated. Riven held that sword.

"Dude! You made it," Riven said. "I was getting worried about you."

He and Sky stood back to back as they fought off more rot monsters.

"I wouldn't be here if it wasn't for Bloom," Sky explained. "She saved me."

"She's way powerful," said Riven. He slashed his energy scimitar through a slimy beast.

"When this is over, I want to take her out on a *real* date," said Sky. "I'll get her flowers and everything." He stabbed another creature. It fell to pieces in front of him.

"With that kind of power, you had *better* treat her right," Riven joked. "Know what I'm saying?" A giant berserker charged the two heroes. "Watch out, bro!" Riven warned.

The beast raised a hand to strike. A thin blade flashed and its slime-covered hand fell away and dissolved into a thousand bugs.

Behind the beast, Brandon twirled his double spear. "Hey, just thought I'd give you a *hand*." He spun the weapon and finished off the creature.

Two more rot monsters grew in its place. Then two bolts of light flew over Sky's shoulder. The monsters were blown to bits. "Eat that!" yelled Timmy. He aimed his pistol toward the sky and blasted an incoming stingray.

"They just keep coming!" yelled Brandon.

Sky pulled a small device off of his belt. He pressed a button and two small energy blades appeared. "See how you like the Boomerang!" He sailed the small weapon toward the back of a rot monster. The beast split in two. Then it reformed into *two* rot monsters.

"Let me show you how it's done, bro," said Riven. He pulled out two throwing stars. "Double Star!" he said as he whipped the blades toward the beasts. They stuck in the monsters' chests, and then blew up. Slimy bugs showered the heroes.

The insects quickly regrouped and poured into another pile. They climbed over each other, forming the biggest berserker yet.

"Now!" shouted Miss Faragonda.

The boys ducked as Faragonda, Griffin, and Saladin combined their powers and blasted the huge beast. This time, it didn't come back.

"Nicely done," said Sky.

Miss Faragonda sighed. "It doesn't matter. As long as they have the Dragon Fire, the monsters will just keep coming until they wipe us all out."

CHAPTER 31

Icy didn't know how that meddling pixie got her powers back. One thing was for sure: Bloom was going to pay. "You're going to wish you never survived the destruction of Sparks!" she yelled at Bloom.

Icy reached out and pulled the moisture from the air around her. She formed several blocks of ice and hurled them at the floating fairy. The ice slammed around Bloom, creating a jagged ice-box. With all her might, Icy willed Bloom's new prison toward the ground. The box shattered into a million pieces as it struck the forest floor.

"Game over!" Icy laughed.

"Not yet!" said a voice behind her. She turned to see that Bloom had materialized right behind her.

The meddling pixie reared back and punched Icy. The witch saw stars as she toppled downward. When she hit the lake, the wind was knocked out of her. As she sunk beneath the surface, Icy almost lost consciousness. She shook her head to stay awake. Then, while she remained underwater, she created a giant hand out of the surrounding liquid. It reached up and grabbed the hovering fairy. Icy rose out of the water as Bloom was pulled into the lake.

"You're going down!" Icy said as she pulled a wet strand of hair from her face. "I'm going to turn this lake into the Bloom Memorial Ice Rink." She extended a hand and showered the lake with her most powerful freezing spell. The lake cracked as it froze solid. "We'll hold our annual Broom Hockey Smash Bash here."

CHAPTER 32

"**Flora!**" **Stella shouted** as she flew toward the cyclone. She watched as her friend spun around inside. She looked back at Musa and Tecna. "Come on!"

Instead of fleeing from the terrible tornado, the fairies headed straight for it. Stella led the way as they tore through the wall of wind, piercing the giant funnel.

Flying as steady as she could, Stella zipped toward Flora. "Hold on!" she yelled. Flapping her wings wildly, she pushed toward her friend. Finally, she grabbed Flora's hand. "Gotcha!"

Stella reached her hand toward the others. "We have to link our powers! Grab on!" The four fairies grasped each other's hands and held tight. "Let's try that spell from gym class," Stella suggested.

"Oh, yeah," said Musa.

"Perfect," agreed Tecna.

They closed their eyes and combined their energy. They

began to glow like a giant fireball. They chanted: "*Turn our Winx into a giant wall. Bounce off of us like a rubber ball!*"

Stella felt the spell working. She opened her eyes to see the cyclone leave them and head right for Darcy and Stormy.

Darcy shielded herself. "Help!"

The tornado engulfed the witches. It tossed them around like two rag dolls.

"This calls for a flying dungeon spell," said Miss Griffin, on the ground below. Along with Faragonda and Saladin, they shot a bright beam of light toward the two witches. The energy stripped away the cyclone and enveloped Darcy and Stormy. A giant spiked ball formed around them. The ball fell and slammed into the ground below.

Stella and the others landed beside the three professors.

"Nice work!" said Flora.

"You, too!" said Griffin.

"Look," said Faragonda. She pointed to the attacking beasts. Several of the monsters screamed and vanished into thin air. "Darcy and Stormy's monsters are disappearing!"

"But Icy still has hoards of them," Griffin pointed out.

CHAPTER 33

Icy hovered over the frozen lake a bit longer. *It couldn't be that easy*, she thought. *Could it?* A cracking sound told her it wasn't. Giant fissures appeared in the ice. They spiderwebbed across the lake. Then . . . *BOOM!*

Jagged ice flew into the air as the center of the lake exploded. Bloom flew out and hovered above the water. She glared at Icy.

"Go ahead, flap your little wings and cop your little princess 'tude," Icy taunted. "I'm going to summon *all* of my Dragon Fire power for one final strike!"

Icy concentrated on the very heart of the Dragon Fire itself. She felt the power coursing through her veins as she prepared to deal the final blow. Icy smiled as she willed all of the water in the lake to rise into the air. Shafts of liquid froze into ice shards and hurled toward Bloom. They slammed against her as if she were a magnet and they were spikes of steel. Icy laughed as more and more piled onto the fairy. They crashed on top of each other until a jagged mountain of ice stood where the lake had been.

Icy cackled proudly. "And the winner is . . . me! Was there ever any doubt?" She began to fly back to Alfea. "Enjoy the rest of your frozen, frigid life."

She heard a distant roar. "No," she said to herself. Icy turned and saw an enormous dragon of fire appear at the base of the mountain. It slowly coiled around the structure until it reached the top. It began to glow and the mountain began to rumble. "No," Icy repeated.

Ka-VOOOOOOM!

The mountain exploded and Icy tumbled backwards. Glowing bright orange, Bloom hovered where the mountain once stood. The fairy was so bright, Icy had to shield her eyes. Bloom spread her fingertips as she gathered energy around her. The wind flew past Icy as it was sucked toward the fairy. She glowed brighter than ever.

"You're done," Bloom said calmly.

She fired a blinding column of fire toward Icy.

"NO!" Icy yelled.

CHAPTER 34

Stella battled two rot monsters at once. She leapt over one as it swung at her with its jagged claw. She slammed it in the head with her scepter, and then landed behind it. While the first monster recovered, the second one charged. Stella powered up her scepter, ready to blast it. Then, something unexpected happened. The beast wailed, and then disappeared. Stella looked around the battlefield. More monsters vanished.

"That monster just disappeared," said Faragonda.

"*All* of the monsters are disappearing," said Stella. "It can only mean one thing." She held her scepter over her head in triumph. "Bloom's kicking Icy's booty!"

Musa sat up off the ground. Riven reached down to help her up. "Need a hand?"

Musa looked up and smiled. "Yo."

Tecna walked over to Timmy as he holstered his pistol. "Hey, Timmy," said Tecna.

Timmy nervously adjusted his glasses. "Uh . . . Hi, Tecna."

Stella felt a hand on her shoulder. "Hey, princess," said Brandon.

Stella turned and smiled. "Hey."

Flora pointed to the sky. "Look, the sun's coming out!"

Everyone smiled as they watched the black clouds fade away. Once again, the sun radiated over Alfea. Then Stella noticed a small silhouette against the bright sky. The shape grew larger. Soon, Stella knew exactly who it was.

"Bloom!" yelled Musa.

Her wings fluttered as Bloom approached. She held an unconscious Icy in her arms. As she lightly touched down, Bloom gently set the witch on the ground. Icy moaned softly but didn't wake up.

"You did it, Bloom!" said Flora.

"You rule!" said Stella.

"I am so happy you're all okay," said Bloom. Kiko dashed through everyone's legs and leapt into Bloom's arms. She wiped a tear from her eye. "It's so good to see you guys."

Sky stepped forward. "Bloom, you were awesome!"

Chapter 35

Bloom watched as the guards placed the magic restraint around Icy's forehead. Even though the three witches were weak from their defeat, they seemed angrier than ever. Once they were beaten, the city of Magix had returned to normal. Miss Griffin contacted the authorities there and they came to retrieve the witches.

"I made a big mistake letting those witches into Cloud Tower," Griffin told Faragonda.

"It's not your fault," assured Faragonda.

Griffin sighed. "Perhaps the time has come for me to retire."

Miss Faragonda placed a hand on her shoulder. "Listen, I may not agree with everything that you teach at Cloud Tower, but I do know that you're the best in your field. You can't quit, Griffy," said Faragonda.

Miss Griffin smiled. "Well, I really do love my job. Maybe I just have to get more campus security and reevaluate the admissions process."

Griffin glared at the three witches. "I've thought a lot about what to do with them, and I've decided to send them to Do Gooders Boot Camp." She grinned. "That will sweeten the evil out of them."

Miss Faragonda tried to stifle a laugh. "I hear everything there is terribly cute."

"It is," Griffin confirmed. "They're going to be absolutely miserable."

Everyone watched as the guards escorted Darcy and Stormy through a small portal.

"Bye!" Stella said with a wave.

Just before Icy was escorted through, she turned and glared at Bloom. "I am *so* not done with you!"

Once she disappeared through the swirling portal, Pepe ran after her. He hopped through just as the portal vanished. The strange sight made everyone laugh. Everyone was amused but Kiko. Bloom saw that he was going to miss his new friend. Bloom picked him up and gave him a hug.

That night, as the party was in full swing, Bloom sat by the well and looked at the stars. She would go back to her friends soon. She just needed some time alone to sit and think. From the sound of things, everyone was having a wonderful time.

Miss Griffin and the rest of the witches didn't stay. They returned to Cloud Tower. Miss Griffin made it clear that they didn't go to fairy parties; they crashed them. It seemed as if she was back to her usual self. However, Mirta was allowed to stay. She was going to be the first witch-exchange student. She couldn't wait to learn things that they didn't teach at Cloud Tower. Maybe she could teach Bloom and her friends something new as well.

Speaking of cultural exchange, Knut stayed behind as well. He was going to be the new Alfea custodian. Flora offered to make him a magical herbal shampoo that would help with his O.B.O. (ogre body odor).

"Hey, there you are," said a familiar voice. "I was looking for you."

"I just needed some fresh air," said Bloom.

Sky sat beside her. "Are you okay?"

"I don't know," Bloom replied. "I started thinking about how summer's about to start and everyone's going away for a couple of months and I got really sad." She leaned her head on his shoulder. "This is going to sound cheesy, but . . . I'll miss you."

"Hey, I'm going miss you, too," Sky said.

Bloom lifted her head and looked into his blue eyes. They stared at each other for a moment. Then, they closed their eyes and lightly kissed. It was incredible.

Sky slowly leaned back and stammered a bit. "But . . . uh . . . the school year's not over yet."

Bloom was a bit light-headed. "Yeah . . . uh . . . that's right."

Sky stood and held out a hand. "We still have time to dance. Want to get back to the party?"

Bloom looked into his eyes once more and smiled.

"Yeah. Okay." She took his hand and they walked back to the party.

Bloom and Sky sat at the long table with all her friends. They ate great food, drank delicious milkshakes, and talked about what they were going to do next year. Even all of the professors seemed to have a great time.

Miss Faragonda stood near the end of the table and raised a hand. Everyone stopped talking and turned to the school's headmistress. "This has been a unique year," she said, "capped by a day of extraordinary courage. You certainly behaved like true Alfea girls. In fact, you did so well, I feel it unnecessary to have final exams this year. You're all passing with honors!"

The girls cheered.

"All right, now that this is settled . . ." She pretended to dance. "It's time to par-tay!" Everyone laughed and clapped.

"This is the best party ever," said Flora.

"Yeah," Mirta agreed. "Fairy parties are not so bad."

Bloom stood. "I'd like to propose a toast." She raised her milkshake. "To friends!"

"To *new* friends!" Knut added.

Sky glanced at Riven. "To old friends."

Brandon raised his glass and turned to Stella. "And to princesses."

Stella raised a finger. "Let's toast nonroyal people, too," she giggled. "We can't forget about them."

Tecna stood. "And to Bloom!"

"Yeah!" cheered Musa. "A special shout-out to Bloom!"

"When she got here, she didn't even have wings," Stella announced. "And today she saved the whole realm!"

"To Bloom!" everyone said in unison.

Bloom could feel herself blush. "You guys!"

"You know," said Flora, "we're going to be sophomores next year!"

"And, you know what they say," Stella added. "Sophomore year is even more thrilling and more exciting than the first year!"

Bloom raised her glass high. "To next year!"